AN HONORABLE MAN?

Annabel arched an eyebrow. "Why did you come, Major?"

"To see how you are faring," Justin replied. "Also to express my condolences for the loss of your father."

She cast him a searching look. "Are those your sole reasons for calling?"

Justin flushed and dropped his gaze. He'd come because he couldn't bear the thought of leaving for Lisbon without knowing if Annabel returned his sentiments. He rose to his feet.

"I came because you haunt my dreams. I came because I wish to court you."

Annabel's jaw dropped. "Are you mad? I'm in mourning."

"Rest easy. I do not intend to begin courting you this instant. But before we are a minute older, I mean to find out if the feelings I have for you are mutual."

Before she could utter a word of protest, Justin pulled her to her feet and boldly embraced her. The instant his lips claimed hers Annabel was caught up in a powerful current of pleasurable sensations. When he finally lifted his mouth from hers, she whimpered in protest.

"Y-you kissed me," Annabel said.

"So I did. Tell the truth. Did you like it?"

"Y-yes, but . . . it is most improper!"

He kissed the tip of her elegant nose. "You have me there, sweetheart. However, I meant no disrespect. Will you write to me, Annabel?"

Phylis Warady

Breach of Honor

ZEBRA BOOKS
KENSINGTON PUBLISHING CORP.

ZEBRA BOOKS are published by

Kensington Publishing Corp.
850 Third Avenue
New York, NY 10022

First Printing: October, 1995

Printed in the United States of America

This novel is dedicated to my youngest grandson.
Welcome to the world, Kyle Joseph.
May the road always rise up to meet you.
May the wind always be at your back.

One

London 1812

Annabel Drummond bustled into the breakfast room of the town house in Russell Square. As usual, her father had his nose buried inside the financial section of the *London Times*. Arms akimbo, she'd wager a groat that the periodical at his elbow was none other than Lloyd's List of Imports and Exports.

Amused by his predictability, she was still smiling when she said, "Good morning, Papa."

Angus Drummond lowered the newspaper to scowl at his daughter. "You are dressed to go oot. Rather early to be abroad, you ken."

Annabel's smile faded as she warily examined his glum frogish features. Her gaze lingered on his undershot jawline embellished with gray side whiskers grown, she'd long suspected, to obscure heavy jowls that bracketed his mouth. Instead the whiskers served as physical evidence of his stubbornly willful nature.

Father would persist in trying to browbeat her, thought Annabel. But he'd catch cold at that. She was hardly a green lass. At four and twenty, she was made of sterner stuff.

Assuming a bland mask that hid a nature equally as obstinate as the dour Scotsman's, she calmly donned her gloves. "It is early," she admitted. "But since you insist upon a fish course for your guests, I must hie to Billinsgate before this morning's catch is picked over."

"Och, I'd forgotten about tonight's dinner party. Weel, dinna let me keep you, lass."

Annabel started to go, then hesitated. "I plan to take the carriage. Unless you need it, of course."

"Nae, take it. I dinna plan to stir from the house taday."

With that, Angus raised his newspaper, discouraging further conversation. That was fine with Annabel. She had errands to run and was eager to be off.

Even so, it was not until the coachman turned onto High Holburn that her depression lifted. Indeed, when younger, knowing she could never measure up to her father's expectations had hurt her feelings. But now, after seven years of serving as his housekeeper, she recognized there was no pleasing him and had long since given up trying to engage his affections.

Annabel slipped her hand from her fur muff and plucked a bit of lint from her stylishly-cut pelisse of rust-colored merino, fastened with black braided claws. Dressing in the highest kick of fashion was her sole vanity. Or at least the only one she was willing to own up to, she conceded with a wry grin.

She sobered. She was not being entirely fair. Although irascible and frugal by nature, her father was not a complete ogre. He did provide her with an adequate clothing allowance and pin money. So who was she to complain?

Annabel reached up to readjust the rakish tilt of her Britannia hat, which matched her oversized, pearl gray fur muff. Permitting herself a wintry smile, she blessed the day she'd found a clever dressmaker in the Strand, thus enabling her to indulge her penchant for style and quality of fabric, whilst at the same time setting aside a sizable chunk of her clothing allowance to finance an occasional flyer in the stock market. For, to her credit, she was every bit as canny in regard to money matters as her father, who'd amassed a respectable fortune with his fleet of merchant ships.

Godfrey Camden, tenth Earl of Summerfield, was nine and three quarters minutes late for his appointment. "Curse him!" muttered Angus Drummond. Being a belted earl dinna give him license to abuse an honest tradesman. Aristocrat or no!

Hands linked behind his back, the Scotsman paced the length of the worn Wilton carpet. He was in the room he'd appropriated seven years ago as his private domain, right after he'd moved bag and baggage into the fashionable Georgian town house in Russell Square.

The ruts in his furrowed brow deepened as he reversed his direction. The town house had been willed to Annabel, a mere seventeen at the time, by Lady Winthrop, her maternal grandmother. But, as far as he was concerned, the haughty harridan's generous gesture was spoiled by her failure to bequeath an adequate sum of money for its upkeep. Thus, while he never missed a chance to take advantage of the fashionable location, he deeply resented having to shell out any of his hardearned groats to keep the premises up to snuff. Even more aggravating, despite diligent efforts to transfer ownership from his daughter to himself, he'd met with dismal failure. Though heaven knows he'd tried. But the trust deed appeared to have no loopholes, thanks, no doubt, to the wily shylock who'd drawn up his mother-in-law's airtight will.

Angus's ruminations were interrupted by his taciturn

butler, who entered to announce Lord Summerfield's arrival.

"Weel, dinna stand there like a slug. Show the mon in."

Once Fenton left, Angus, eager to seize the advantage, faced the room's entrance. Watching Summerfield saunter across the threshold, he reflected that while he and Godfrey Camden had been classmates at Edinburgh, their reacquaintance was quite recent.

"Rather a chilly day don't you agree?" asked the earl as he wrung the Scotsman's hand.

"Och, it be bonny enough weather for February—or so I ken."

The earl's genial smile slipped a fraction. Jet black locks liberally salted with gray framed a flushed, dissipated face that retained tantalizing hints of former good looks.

While aggravated that Summerfield offered no apology for his tardiness, Angus held his peace. "Have a chair whilst I pour you a wee dram of Scotch whiskey to ward off your chill."

Slumped with indolent grace upon a padded wing chair, the earl accepted the tumbler his host offered and which, after only a few sips, he pronounced, "Excellent whiskey."

His protuberant brown eyes coolly remote, Angus waved the compliment aside. "Now then, Summerfield, shall we get down to business?"

The earl nervously ran a hand through his salt and pepper locks. "If you say so."

"Weel, I do sae so. So get on with it, mon."

"Very well. To be blunt, I'm dashed short of the ready to make needed improvements at my family seat. Improvements that my bailiff assures me will eventually put the land back in good heart so it can once again turn a profit. So here I am, Angus, come with hat in hand to ask for money."

The Scotsman awarded his visitor a sardonic smile. His guess as to why Summerfield had come sniffing around him had been right on the mark.

"Owning a fleet of merchant ships, it stands to reason you're flush in the pocket. Why not grant me a loan for old time's sake. There's a good chap!"

Angus shook his head. "Nae. My bailiwick be the sea not the land. I wad likely end up losing my shirt. And wad deserve to for investing in something I dinna ken more about than a wee bairn."

Summerfield's smile faltered as he rose to his feet. "No harm in asking, I trust?"

Angus shrugged. " 'Tis nae great matter."

The earl sighed. "The moneylenders are hot on my trail. You wouldn't happen to know a rich heiress amenable to a whirlwind courtship, would you?"

Drummond's sardonic smirk emphasized the prominent jowls he was at pains to hide behind fluffy side whiskers.

"Dare I presume from the odd way you are regarding me that you've someone in mind I might court?" asked the earl.

Angus cast him a sly look. "Mayhap I do. But I need a wee bit of time to mull things over."

Summerfield made an impatient gesture. "Time? I've precious little to spare before my creditors see me tossed into debtor's prison."

The Scotsman's thoughts raced. Apart from his penchant to pinch pennies, his sole ambition was to rise above his humble origins. What better way to do this than to provide Annabel with a large enough dowry to buy a title?

"Are you free to dine here this evening?"

Ever suave, the earl drawled laconically, "It will be my pleasure."

"Gude. We dine at eight. Dinna be late."

The Drummond coach bowled past the august Bank of England, popularly nicknamed the Old Lady of Threadneedle Street. Annabel compressed her lips into a thin tight line.

Nathan Rothschild had sent round a note that morning warning cotton futures were destined to drop several notches and advising her to unload the stock she owned in a Manchester mill at once. Which meant that despite her overcrowded schedule, she must somehow squeeze in a flying visit to her man of business.

She glanced at the Friday-faced female seated opposite and wished to heaven she'd left the servant at home. If it were possible, she'd travel on to Billingsgate wharf herself. But this afternoon must be spent back in Russell Square getting ready for tonight's banquet.

Annabel gave a frustrated sigh. Twice a year her father chose to discharge his social obligations with a sumptuous dinner. Indeed, he positively relished confounding business associates long inured to his clutch-fisted manner of conducting daily transactions by treating them to a lavish meal.

Which meant she had only two hours to resolve the urgent matter that required her presence in the heart of the financial district. Thus, knowing her father would be livid if there were no fish course, she'd picked Hadley to go to Billingsgate wharf in her place, chiefly because, in Annabel's opinion, she was the only kitchen maid canny enough not to get rooked by the sly fishmongers. But now, Hadley was balking. She claimed it was not seemly for Miss Annabel to be wandering about the city without even a footman to lend her countenance.

Annabel's troubled ruminations ceased when the coachman drew to a halt before the Royal Exchange, which consisted of two U-shaped buildings arranged to form a square. Alighting, she waited until she saw the Drummond coach pull back into traffic before she entered the spacious inner courtyard.

Inside, she was content to remain hidden in the shadows created by an upper gallery directly above her head while she studied the milling throng. By and large, the crowd was made of gentlemen clad in the somber browns and blacks favored by stock brokers, solicitors and bankers. However, there were a few ladies strolling about the courtyard as well. Annabel drew comfort from their presence, since the very last thing she desired was to call attention to herself as an oddity.

She scarcely glanced at the series of handsome Roman arches that supported the upper gallery of the brownstone structure as she crossed the courtyard. Scant minutes later, she slipped inside the office of her man of business, Kenneth Boswell.

The room stood empty save for his clerk.

"Good day, Nigel. Where's Mr. Boswell?"

The clerk, who'd been sitting hunched over a ledger, jumped down off his high stool and bowed. "At Lloyd's Coffee House. Why? Do you have an appointment?"

She shook her head. "Nevertheless, I'd like a word with him. Do you expect him back soon?"

"I couldn't venture to guess. He's with a client."

"I see." She thought for a minute longer, then added, "I'm in something of a hurry today, yet it's imperative I speak to him. Be so good as to nip upstairs and advise him of my presence."

The clerk's long, thin face took on a hunted expression. "Oh, miss, much as it pains me to disoblige you, I dare not leave my post."

Annabel experienced a strong temptation to ring a peal over the unfortunate clerk's head. She was soon able to abandon the idea on the grounds that giving vent to her temper was unwarranted and would undermine her dignity.

Instead, she announced huffily, "Very well, then. I shall see to the matter myself."

Major Justin Camden, on convalescent leave from Craufurd's Light Division, sat with his back against the wall of the booth closest to the entrance. His eyes reflected shrewd intelligence as they cast furtive glances about Lloyd's Coffee Room.

Seated opposite, Kenneth Boswell awarded the major an exasperated look. "For God's sake, Justin, cease darting suspicious looks into every booth. It's downright embarrassing."

The major's pale blue eyes were in stark contrast to the jet black curls that framed a handsome face, tanned several shades darker than the English taste by the Portuguese sun. His friendship with Boswell dated back to when they were both schoolboys.

"My deepest apologies, old chap. It's a maneuver that saved my hide countless times on the Peninsula."

"Doubtless it did. But you're safe as houses here at Lloyd's."

"I realize that. Still it's a hard habit to break."

"Quite!" Boswell wrinkled his brow. "Even more baffling is your determination to rejoin your regiment. After your leg wound at Almeida, I should think you'd be ready to cry quits."

The major aimed an incredulous look at his former school chum. "What? Miss all the excitement?"

Justin's gaze burned with intensity as he recalled the battle of Fuentes de Onoro in which he'd had the honor of participating in the rescue of the crippled Seventh, temporarily trapped behind French lines until Wellington ordered the major's commanding officer, General Robert Craufurd, to go in and bring back the broken battalions.

"Sell out? Never!"

"You shall have to if your loss of mobility is permanent, will you not?"

Trust Boswell to go for his Achilles heel, Justin thought sourly. "What a morbid fellow you are, Kenneth. First off, you insist I make up a will in case I die serving my country. Then you try to cut up my peace by hinting my leg won't mend properly. Pure fustian, my friend. The surgeon assures me I can soon trade in my crutches for a cane."

"Morbid? Ha! Unlike you, I've no stomach for carnage. Give me a fusty old brief any day. Which reminds me. Do you wish to carry on your person a copy of the will you signed before witnesses?"

Owning so little, the major had hardly thought a will necessary. Boswell's genuine shock that he hadn't prepared one already had persuaded him that perhaps a will was necessary, after all.

"No. It is safer in your keeping."

"Very well, I'll file it away. Now then, when does the surgeon say you may throw away your crutches?"

Justin sighed. "He refuses to be pinned down. But whenever it is, it cannot be too soon for me."

"I confess I don't understand you at all, Justin. Imagine wishing to plunge right back into danger after your close scrape."

"Somebody has to defend England from Napoleon." The major smiled faintly. "Besides, I consider it an honor to serve under Wellington."

"To be sure, Arthur Wellesley's star is on the rise. However, I would remind you that you are heir presumptive to an earldom. You ought to think twice about returning to the battlefield."

Justin responded to the solicitor's reasoning with a derisive snort. "Gammon! At five-and-forty, the present earl is hale and hearty. Ergo, despite a somewhat dissolute lifestyle, I expect he'll soon marry and beget a more direct heir than a mere distant cousin. Nor do I envy Godfrey his title. Army life suits me."

Two

"More coffee?" asked Justin.

"None for me, thanks." Kenneth Boswell scooted across his bench and stood up. "Excuse me for a nonce. I see an insurance broker I must needs have a word with."

The major gave a dismissive wave of his hand. "By all means tootle off. I did not mean to monopolize your time."

Boswell looked conscience-stricken. "Don't talk rot. I always enjoy your company."

Justin responded with a bark of laughter. "And I yours. Yet our business is done. Nor am I your only client."

"Just so. Still I don't like to desert you."

The major shot him an exasperated look. "Spare me your crocodile tears. Begone so I can enjoy my coffee in peace."

Once Boswell scuttled off, Justin lifted a steaming mug to his lips and drank in its aroma. Umm! The strong scent was so sublime he almost sighed aloud. As for its taste, it put to shame what passed for coffee in the wilds of Portugal. Compared to that bilge, Lloyd's fresh roasted coffee was ambrosia fit for the gods.

He ventured a sip and received a scalded tongue for his pains. Eyes watering, he ruefully admitted it served him right for not letting it cool off first. He plunked his mug back down on the wooden table and glanced about the vast room seeking a diversion.

He espied Kenneth Boswell chatting with a soberly-dressed gentleman but saw no one else he recognized. It came as no surprise. At home in an army barracks, here at the Royal Exchange, where the bulk of the city's financial transactions took place, Justin was out of his element.

His restless gaze had almost traveled full circle before he spotted the girl of his dreams. Her willowy figure smartly-attired in a rust-colored pelisse, she stood framed in the archway that separated the coffee room from the Exchange's upper gallery. Enchanted by this vision of femininity, his throat tightened. And although he'd been taught from the cradle that staring was rude, he couldn't bring himself to look elsewhere. Instead, he drank in her essence like a man dying of thirst.

Springy titian ringlets peeped out from the edges of her pearl gray fur hat to frame an oval face enhanced by a peaches and cream complexion. The distance between them made it impossible to tell the exact color of her eyes but, if he'd had to guess, Justin would have said they were brown. Not that it mattered. Whatever their color, he was in the throes of instant infatuation.

It was something he'd never before experienced! Something he'd never believed in. Something he was not sure he believed in even now—despite the fact that he'd been poleaxed by a perfect stranger.

Telling himself the sooner he broke out of the spell of enthrallment the better, he tore his gaze from hers and, picking up his mug, drained it. His pale blue eyes resolutely refocused upon businessmen seated in the booths on the far side of the coffee room.

Yet despite Herculean efforts to resist the appealing baggage's lures, he found he could not entirely ignore her compelling presence. In short, his was a hopeless case.

At point-non-plus, Justin was uncertain of what defensive measures to take. He could leave of course. But in order to do so, he must brush past her. He frowned. Just who was he trying to fool? What saved him from disgracing himself was his bum leg. It rendered him incapable of giving way to his crack-brained impulse to snatch her up and carry her off like the Vikings had in medieval times.

No question his sense of honor was being tested, just as his mettle had often been tested in battle. His best bet, he finally decided, would be to study the auburn-haired siren the same way Wellington had studied the French long before engaging them in battle.

Feeling more in command of himself now that he had a definite strategy in mind, Justin recast his gaze in her direction. The intent way she peered into the crowd made him suspect she sought someone in particular. A sweeping glance about the room convinced him of the futility of trying to pinpoint the object of her quest. It could be either her solicitor or her man of business. Or her husband, father or brother. Or even her lover.

Perish the thought! A husband would be bad enough. A lover, he could not stomach. Justin gave a mirthless chuckle. So much for idle conjecture. Whatever her quest, it was actually none of his business.

Yet, he wanted it to be! Never before had he felt so vulnerable, or so befuddled. Fearful for his own sanity, he gazed at her suspiciously. But the longer he looked, the more bemused his expression became.

One dainty hand clutched a ridiculously-oversized fur muff that matched her hat; the other's knuckles rested saucily on her hip. One shapely foot molded in kid leather tapped the floor boards. The major was unable to suppress a grin. Obviously, patience was not the lady's long suit.

A sudden twinge of pain made him wince. He could hardly wait for the day he no longer suffered discomfort, or the day his leg no longer stiffened up because he'd sat too long in one spot. He glared at the pair of crutches he'd propped against the back wall of the booth. Truth be told, he hated having to use those cursed wooden sticks, but had no other choice if he wished to be mobile.

Justin gently massaged his aching thigh. He should leave before the pain got worse. But pride was stronger than common sense. He'd rather die than hobble past her on crutches. Nothing could be more humiliating than for her to regard him as a helpless cripple.

"I say, old man, I'm on my way back to my office. Can I give you a hand with the stairs?" asked Boswell.

Although the offer was tempting, Justin's dread of being reduced to an object of pity in the flame-haired beauty's eyes was stronger. However, a surreptitious glance toward the archway revealed that she'd vanished. Stunned by his sharp sense of loss, he bit his tongue to keep from crying out in protest.

Boswell held up his hand. "No arguments. Can't have you taking a tumble, can I?"

Justin manfully swallowed his pride. "Actually, I'd appreciate a sturdy shoulder to lean on. Hand me my crutches, there's a friend."

Once they'd been moved within arm's reach, the major rose, and balancing his weight on one foot, positioned a crutch under each armpit.

His thoughts morose, Justin set off at a slow hobble. Today he'd been on his feet too long and his leg ached like the devil. He should have left Lloyd's long since— regardless of the poor impression he might make on some nameless chit, especially as chances were they'd probably never meet again. Just as chances were they'd have nothing in common if they did.

At the head of the stairs, Justin glanced all the way to the bottom and almost lost his nerve. What on earth had possessed him to climb up here in the first place? Not that his reason mattered greatly. What mattered was that these stairs were his only means of return to ground level. And the sooner he started his descent, the sooner he could breathe easier.

By the time he was halfway down, his uniform was soaked with sweat and his good leg was trembling so badly he worried it would collapse beneath him. Yet he dared not pause to rest for fear some stock broker in a tearing hurry might accidentally nudge him off balance. Justin gritted his teeth and pressed doggedly onward.

Sweat poured off him in rivulets by the time he stood at the foot of the stairs. Tempted to send up a rousing cheer, he was too done up to muster the wind.

Boswell, who'd had the grace to hold his tongue during the difficult descent, now cast him an anxious glance. "Wait here while I summon a cab."

The solicitor turned to go, only to find his path blocked by the same red-headed charmer. Justin stood suddenly straighter and his eyes were bright.

But the titian-haired beauty took scant notice of the gleam in Justin's eye. Her gaze was fixed on the solicitor. "Kenneth Boswell, I've been looking high and low for you."

A slow grin transformed the solicitor's pasty features. "My dear Miss Drummond, what a welcome breath of fresh air you are amongst all these sobersides."

"Never you mind trying to turn me up sweet, sir. It is imperative I speak to you."

The major shot her a look of approval. He honestly felt Boswell had made an ass of himself by laying on the flattery with a trowel. Evidently, so had Miss Drummond.

The solicitor frowned. "My schedule is quite crowded today. Cannot you come back tomorrow?"

Justin smiled to himself as he filed away her family name for future reference. He'd guessed wrong about the color of her eyes. They were not brown. They were dark blue. Still, he'd been right about her fiery temper. Once again she was tapping the toe of her kid leather half-boot and, judging by her flushed cheeks, a barely banked passion hovered just beneath a thin veneer of civility.

He grimaced. Much as he would like to stick around for the fireworks, his bum leg hurt too much to dawdle. He'd best be on his way while he was still ambulatory.

"Miss Drummond, your servant." The major glanced at his friend. "I'll say goodbye to you here, old chap."

Boswell snorted. "Don't be daft. In a word, you're done up." He turned to Annabel. "Miss Drummond, I shall see you in my office directly after I've snabbled a hackney for the major. I trust that is satisfactory."

"Quite!" she snapped.

Justin scarcely noted the solicitor's departure. He was too busy observing the play of emotions on the disgruntled beauty's countenance. Evidently she expected Boswell to bend over backward whenever she snapped her fingers. Justin struggled to contain his amusement at her naivete. But it was no use. A chuckle escaped and, even though he tried to cover it with a cough, she was too perceptive to be taken in.

"Laugh at me, will you?" she fumed. "If I had my parasol, I'd be tempted to knock your block off."

He cast her a roguish grin. "Would you, little spitfire? I should so enjoy disarming you."

Trembling with fury, she stamped her foot. "You, sir, are abominable. I do not intend to put up with you laughing up your sleeve another minute!"

Annabel spun on her heel so fast she almost lost her balance. Halfway through her about-face, her oversized muff struck one of Justin's crutches. It flew out from under his armpit and hit the paved courtyard with a resounding clatter.

"Devil a bit!" he exclaimed.

Pivoting, Annabel's lovely face reflected horrified amazement as she witnessed the major's frantic attempt to regain his balance. His arms flailing impotently, he waged a desperate, last-ditch effort to retain his footing. But with only one leg to support him, it was not too surprising that he ended up sprawled on the courtyard floor.

Bedazed, the sound made on impact echoed and re-choed in Justin's ears. He'd landed so hard on the baked-clay surface, every bone in his body was jarred. He'd tried to cushion his fall, but obviously he'd failed miserably.

"Oh no!" cried Annabel. Heedless of her stylish ensemble, she dropped to her knees beside him. "Speak to me, sir. Are you in pain?"

Pain? He groaned. There were no words to describe it. Nonetheless, his pain was inconsequential compared to his humiliation. It was bad enough having to hobble about on crutches in her presence; far worse to end up in an ignoble heap at her feet. The mere thought of his sorry showing threatened to unman him.

"Stupid question," she chided herself. "You fell like a ton of bricks. You must be in terrible pain."

Actually, his entire body ached. However, excruciating pains emanating from his game leg were the hardest to bear stoically. Deciding to test the waters, he opened one eye.

"Tell me where you hurt the most," she pleaded, her gaze soft with sympathy.

Stung by the pity he read in her gaze, Justin responded with a sardonic chuckle. "Why? Do you plan to kiss it better?"

Annabel, who was in no mood to be teased, bristled. "Sir, this is no time to be playing the jester."

"Quite right! I seem to have twisted my wrist. While you kiss it well, I shall compile a list of all my aches and pains. Does that please you?"

"Please me?" Clearly incensed, she scrambled to her feet. "Beyond a shred of doubt, you, sir, are a buffoon of the first order. You have put me in such a passion that if you were standing, I'd knock you down."

"My dear Miss Drummond," Justin drawled. "On the odd chance it may have escaped your notice, allow me to assure you, you already have."

Three

That evening found Annabel seated at the foot of the dinner table, wearing a white lace over white satin evening gown, the fashionably-low neckline exposing a bit more bosom than she felt comfortable baring.

Even more aggravating, she kept lapsing into a brown study. Never mind that she was the hostess, her thoughts were preoccupied by the proud soldier who'd ended up sprawled at her feet. The despair in his pale blue eyes seemed indelibly etched in her memory, which struck her as nothing short of remarkable, given that she'd been in such a blasted hurry to sell her cotton futures before the market dropped further, she'd paid scant notice to his humiliation. Perversely, now that it was too late to gracefully make amends, his odd-colored eyes haunted her.

She owed him an apology. Never mind that she did not know his name. She could always worm it out of Kenneth Boswell. However, she drew the line at traipsing all over London in search of him. Nothing for it. She must expunge the incident from her mind and trust that, given time, her guilt would fade.

"A penny for your thoughts, my pretty," murmured the Earl of Summerfield.

Startled by his amorous tone, she regarded him warily. His pale blue eyes reminded her of the major's, except that the earl's were bloodshot. Confound it! She'd let her thoughts wander again. She must be on her guard. She must not dwell on her morning encounter. She must concentrate on this dinner party.

All, save one, of the guests were acquaintances of long standing. The sole exception was Summerfield, whom her father had insisted upon inviting at the last minute. His rank dictated that Annabel juggle the place cards until he ended up in the chair beside her.

Gazing from between thick, curly, auburn lashes, she studied his haughty profile, still mystified as to why her father had insisted upon including him in a dinner party of businessmen. For that matter, surely the earl had known he'd be a fish out of water, so why had he come?

Painfully thin, his face resembled a road map, depicting steady erosion of once-handsome features. Further signposts of an habitual imbiber were a ruddy complexion and a marked puffiness of facial skin. Still, the life he led was his own business. Her job as hostess was to be civil to *all* Papa's guests. Including this despicable roue whom she'd just caught ogling her bosom!

Mortified, Annabel flushed scarlet and darted a silent appeal to her father, presiding at the head of the table.

What on earth prompted you to invite this rakeshell to dinner, Papa? she asked him silently.

But Angus was too busy making sheep eyes at Sukie McPherson, still a beauty at forty, and Caro Scott, the flighty wife of the captain of his flagship, to pay attention to his daughter's distress. It did not surprise Annabel. She was used to his benign neglect.

The earl's pointed clearing of his throat recalled Annabel to her duties as hostess. "Did you address me, sir?" she asked politely.

He gave an indolent shrug. "A mere pleasantry. Pray don't regard it."

Taking him at his word, Annabel returned her gaze to her father. At any other time, watching her stiff-rumped parent make a cake of himself by flirting with the ladies would have struck her as hilarious. However, the way the earl's bloodshot eyes roamed over her person made her flesh crawl and she felt the need of paternal support.

"Cheer up, lass. Ye look as if the weight of the entire world rests on yer young shoulders," admonished Colin McPherson.

Turning to her left, Annabel awarded him a warm smile. She'd known the McPhersons since she was in leading strings and was fond of them both. Before any of her father's fleet put to sea, he bought insurance from Colin, who was a member of the prestigious Royal Exchange Assurance Corporation.

"So it does, Uncle Colin. Papa will demand my head for washing if dinner does not progress smoothly."

"Then ye may safely stubble yer fears. Yer skill as a hostess is only surpassed by yer beauty."

She playfully rapped his knuckles with her fan. "You, sir, are adept at telling whiskers with a straight face."

McPherson chuckled. "Found me out, have ye, minx?"

Uncle Colin is such a pet, thought Annabel. Thank goodness he was seated beside her. His sunny disposition offset the predatory nobleman flanking her other side.

She transferred her gaze to the butler. Her slight nod set things in train. Under Fenton's sharp eyes, two footmen resplendent in livery her cheeseparing father only let them don on special occasions, served stuffed artichokes and braised tongue swimming in Cumberland sauce. Annabel took advantage of a brief lull in conversation to glance around the table. Satisfied none of the guests wanted for anything, she kept verbal exchanges between herself and the earl blessedly brief throughout the fish course. But as the servants removed the filet of sole duglere, Summerfield had the temerity to run his index finger up her bare arm from wrist to elbow.

Feeling violated, her dark blue eyes blazed. "Do not touch me again, sir," she advised in an icy undertone. "Else I'm liable to stab you with the prongs of my fork and apologize ever so sweetly afterward."

He responded to her threat with a venomous look that chilled her to the bone. Tempted to bolt, only the knowledge that her father would never forgive such a breach of etiquette kept her seated. Fortunately for her taut nerves, the earl's braying laugh made him the cynosure of all eyes.

Annabel could not say for certain why, instead of continuing to bait her, her tormentor lapsed into a sulky silence. But she suspected the palpable animosity emanating from a hostile audience weighed heavily in his decision.

Her reprieve held throughout the main course, which featured side dishes of asparagus and spinach souffle, accompanied by tender medallions of milk-fed veal served with mushrooms sauted in brandy sauce and garnished with parsley.

But Annabel had lost her appetite. It failed to revive even when the creme brulee was served. Never mind that caramel custard usually made her mouth water, she could not swallow a bite. Adding to her bundle of woe, by the time the covers were removed and assorted cheeses, nuts and hothouse grapes appeared, she had developed a blinding headache.

Their midnight rendezvous took place inside his host's private study. It was a bitter-cold night and the Earl of Summerfield, who had the physique of a cadaver, clung close to the blazing hearth. All the dinner guests had long since departed. It would be hypocritical to claim he missed them. He missed Annabel though. Pleading a migraine, the fiery-haired beauty had retired soon after she'd poured tea in the drawing room. Her departure had left him at the mercy of a room full of bloody tradesmen clearly his social inferiors.

With indolent grace, he accommodated his lanky form to the generous folds of a wing chair covered in striped gold satin. He was careful to keep his eyelids at half-mast in order to hide equal parts greed and lust vying for dominance. Much as he coveted the Scotsman's wealth, his daughter was a juicy morsel whom he could hardly wait to school carnally.

Summerfield issued a wintry smile. That he'd assumed Annabel to be an antidote amused him. Though desperate to avoid debtor's prison, he'd resented the notion of having to marry her in order to get his hands on her father's money. Once they'd met though, he'd had a change of heart, and now he could hardly wait to tie the knot.

His host waggled a decanter of aged Scotch whiskey before his eyes. "Ken I top off your glass?"

Summerfield shook his head emphatically. Having consumed more wine than he ought at dinner, he needed to mind his p's and q's. The stakes were too high to negotiate while half sprung. Not only did he need to wring a generous settlement out of the parsimonious Scotsman, but having seen Annabel, he also wanted to have the banns read as soon as possible.

Except for the ticking clock and an occasional shifting log, you could hear a pin drop, he reflected as he darted a sly glance at his would-be benefactor. How much longer did Drummond intend to toy with him?

He longed to plunge into the meat of the matter, but was loath to risk putting Drummond's back up by being too forthright. He gazed into the flickering fire, wondering how best to broach the subject.

" 'Tis time we laid our cards on the table, you ken?"

Subjected to the Scotsman's cold-eyed scrutiny, the earl fought an urge to squirm. "Just so. Shall we flip a coin to see who leads?"

Angus won the toss. Not one to shilly-shally, he said gruffly, "Kept an eye peeled all evening. I ken you fancy my daughter."

The earl gave a languid nod. "Want her for my countess. Provided we can come to terms, of course."

Angus shot Summerfield a searching glance. How large a dowry must he provide in order to buy Annabel a title?

"How does eight thousand pounds sound? Four thousand advanced once the settlement papers are signed, with the final half due immediately after the wedding ceremony."

Summerfield cast him a withering look. "Do you take me for a flat? I know your assets to the penny. Twenty thousand pounds more like."

Vexed, Angus ran his index finger along the inside edge of his suddenly too-tight collar. To pay out such a sum would hamper cash flow. Besides, it went against the grain to part with any more of the ready than strictly necessary. Still, his driving ambition had always been to rise above his station. When he'd eloped with Annabel's mother, he'd thought he had. However, his grandiose plans had come to naught when Lord Winthrop had disowned Sophia.

But why rehash the past? He'd been given another chance. One he dinna intend to muff. Och, he'd see his daughter a countess and hang the cost!

"Ten thousand pounds. Not a penny more!"

"Fifteen," the earl countered.

"Niver!"

"Cursed skinflint!" Summerfield climbed to his feet. "It appears I must seek my heiress in greener pastures."

Grimfaced, Angus stared at his greedy adversary. He could feel opportunity slipping through his fingers. Yet ten thousand pounds were all he could safely spare without hamstringing his shipping business.

The earl bowed coldly. "Pray convey my regrets to Annabel. I was so taken with her beauty, I was prepared to overlook the fact that her father's a merchant. However, I draw the line at selling my noble patrimony too cheaply."

" 'Tis true I'm in trade. But the lass's mother was the daughter of a marquess."

"I must admit that puts the question of her lineage in a better light. Still, ten thousand pounds is not enough to satisfy my creditors and also raise a family in relative comfort. Nor will it provide Annabel with an adequate jointure in the event of my untimely demise."

Angus gave a frustrated sigh. "The only possible way I can up the ante is to pay a third and final installment on the first wedding anniversary."

Summerfield, who'd almost reached the door, called back over his shoulder. "If you'll settle for fifteen, we have a deal."

"Nae, I cannot. Twelve thousand, broken up into three equal payments, is my absolute limit."

"Done!" cried the earl as he swung round to face the canny merchant. "Damn your eyes! You drive a hard bargain."

"Don't fash yourself. Annabel stands to inherit the whole when I slip my cable."

"Provided you don't remarry," came Summerfield's sly rejoinder.

"No chance of that," Angus assured him, then added gruffly, "Mind you take good care of my lass."

Summerfield chuckled. "Rest easy on that score, Drummond. My countess shall want for nothing."

"See that you keep your word, mon, else you'll answer to me," he warned.

Shortly after Angus saw his guest out, the handsome longcase clock with a brass pendulum knelled. Once it subsided, Angus reclaimed the glass of vintage Scotch neglected during the height of the bargaining session. As he sank down into his favorite wing chair, resplendent in gold striped satin, his lips curved in a fond smile. Knowing he dinna like changes, his canny daughter had had his favorite chair recovered in secret, then presented it to him on his forty-sixth birthday, making it impossible for him to refuse the gift. Never mind that against a background of threadbare carpet and tattered velvet drapes—once bright scarlet—the reupholstered chair called attention to the room's genteel shabbiness. What counted the most was Annabel's thoughtfulness.

His dour demeanor softened. How she'd contrived to set aside anything from the funds he granted quarterly to cover household expenses mystified him. Clearly she'd inherited his ability to squeeze pennies until they squealed. Regrettably, she dinna have her mother's English rose beauty. Still, as the lass matured, her looks had gradually improved until it was hard to recall the scrawny, bran-faced figure she'd cut at seventeen.

That spring, her grandmother, Lady Winthrop, had planned to sponsor her comeout, but instead had passed away suddenly. Angus had toyed with the idea of hiring someone with the proper credentials to introduce Annabel to society once her year of mourning was up. But upon further reflection, he'd decided to spare his homely offspring the humiliation of being a wallflower.

So instead of financing her come out, he'd invested his hard-earned cash in shipping, where it stood a better chance to turn a profit. One by one the years had slipped past until now at four-and-twenty Annabel was, for all intents and purposes, on the shelf. Truth be told, he'd felt occasional twinges of guilt because he dinna make more of a push to see her settled. But now, he was glad he hadn't wasted the ready launching her when she'd resembled a gawky colt. Knowing she wouldn't take, it would have been a cruel as well as costly mistake.

With the passage of years, her looks had improved. And while the lass was not precisely a beauty, at tonight's dinner party the earl had scarcely been able to take his eyes off her.

Narrowing his gaze, Angus continued to muse. In his business dealings, more often than not, he relied on his instincts. Tonight, those instincts had informed him of Summerfield's infatuation, despite the pains the nobleman took to downplay his attraction to Annabel until after the dickering over the size of the settlement ended.

Now, Drummond decided, he could afford to rest on his laurels. His daughter's future looked rosy. Thanks to the canny bargain he'd driven with the earl, she'd soon be the Countess of Summerfield.

In high glee, Angus gave a rusty chuckle. He could hardly wait until morning to inform Annabel of her good fortune.

Four

Annabel woke to fresh-baked croissants and a steaming pot of chocolate that made her mouth water. Rising, she stretched her arms ceilingward, marveling that a sound night's sleep had banished her migraine. That was not always the case. She recalled occasions when her head pounded for days on end. Not this time though. Praise be!

Her euphoria faded. The room was freezing. She cast a wistful glance at the cold hearth. A fire to take off the morning chill would be nice. But her father would consider it an unnecessary extravagance and she was loathe to put his back up.

Besides, with someone as obstinate as Papa, subtlety worked better. She plucked a jonquil-colored dressing gown of soft cashmere off the foot of her bed, donning it as she approached a round table placed before french doors in order to catch the morning sun. Seating herself, she poured chocolate into a china cup and buttered a croissant. As she ate, she experienced a sense of tranquility.

Today she had no dinner party to worry about. She need not suffer fools such as the Earl of Summerfield for at least another six months. Nor were there any potential financial crises to vex her. She could afford to adopt a less harried pace.

The door opened and in walked her abigail. "The

master wants to see you in his study the minute you are dressed."

Annabel burst out laughing. Obviously, she'd spoken too soon.

A half hour later, wearing a Spanish blue frock of challis set off by a full ruff of broad lace encircling her neck and edging her cuffs, she approached her father's study. The closer she drew, the more her feet dragged. She was in no mood to put up with one of his tirades. Yet to ignore his summons would be tantamount to waving a red flag in front of an angry bull.

Expression pensive, her front teeth pressed a groove into her lower lip. Past experience having taught her to eschew direct confrontation whenever possible, she'd become adept at quietly going her own way with him none the wiser. Yet his summons had piqued her curiosity. *Whatever had put him in a bustle?* she wondered. Random possibilities sprang to mind. They ran the gamut from praising her talents as a hostess to damning her for retiring early.

Annabel stood poised before the oaken door. Her father held strange notions in regard to the gentler sex. Seldom ill himself, he considered migraines to be a spurious complaint invented by weak-minded females in the hope of evoking undeserved sympathy from the masculine gender.

Entering her father's inner sanctum, Annabel found him gazing out the window. "You wished to see me, Papa?"

Whirling round, he said curtly, "Aye. Have a chair."

Fearing she was in for one of his infamous scolds, she seated herself and folded her hands in her lap. Then, vexed by her show of meek compliance, she forced herself to meet his gaze.

"For all that you dinna resemble your mama, ye be a bonny lass," he admitted gruffly.

Bemused, Annabel stared at him. Unless her ears had deceived her, he'd paid her a compliment. "Papa, it is not like you to offer Spanish coin. Are you feeling all the thing?"

He gave a rusty chuckle. "Dinna fash yourself, lass. I be fit as a flea."

He'd sounded almost kind. Which confused her no end because he was rarely kind, even to her, of whom he was reasonably fond. However, what really made Annabel nervous was an air of expectancy—a premonition that something momentous was about to occur. She stared at her hands, tempted to wring them.

"I've summat to tell you. Summat I trust will please you as much as it pleases me."

The undisguised glee in his voice made Annabel more tense than ever. Though she took pains to hide it even from him, they were constantly at loggerheads. The likelihood that what pleased her father would also please her was abysmal.

Annabel studied him. That Papa had a secret he could barely contain was abundantly apparent. Annabel was tempted to tell him to keep his bloody secret, that she didn't wish to know what he was dying to tell. But she held her tongue, fearing if he held in his secret much longer, he'd explode.

"Mind, I dinna begrudge ye your good fortune."

Annabel blinked. What on earth was he babbling about?

"Word of a Drummond," Angus crowed. "I've arranged a splendid match for you."

In shock, she clutched both chair arms so hard her knuckles bled white. "What? Are you saying I'm to be married?"

"Aye."

Had Papa taken to imbibing in broad daylight? Annabel dismissed such an outlandish notion with an unladylike snort. He was far too canny to make a Jack pudding of himself over spirits.

Her next theory proved even less palatable. Had something gone awry in his cockloft? Had he gone to bed perfectly sane, only to wake a candidate for Bedlam?

"Papa, you cannot be serious. To the best of my knowledge, no one is courting me."

"Ah, there yer oot, lassie! I've received a bona fide offer for your hand."

The migraine Annabel assumed long gone returned with a vengeance. Close on its heels came the unsettling thought that perhaps it were she, not her father, who was mad as May-butter.

"Well for goodness sake tell all before you burst a blood vessel. Who is this paragon wishful of marrying an ape-leader?"

Angus puffed out his barrel chest. "The Earl of Summerfield, that's who. The mon could nae take his eyes off you last night at dinner. Surely you noticed."

Fuming, Annabel erupted from her chair. "What? Marry that randy rooster? Never!"

Angus's jaw dropped. He'd thought she'd be dancing a jig. Instead, she was chewing nails. His shoulders sagged. If he lived to be a hundred, he'd never understand the workings of the female mind.

" 'Tis nae every day one gets a chance to become a countess. Dinna toss it away."

Annabel struggled to contain the temper she'd inherited from her father. She had no intention of marrying anyone—much less a man she neither trusted nor respected. Yet she must be practical. Succumbing to a fit of hysterics would not help her. Her only hope of persuading her father to abandon this mad course was to air her views calmly.

"Papa, I care nothing for titles. Furthermore, I am convinced the earl and I will not suit."

The Scotsman's protuberant eyes looked ready to pop. "Dinna be daft. Once ye calm doon, you'll sing a different tune."

Annabel could almost feel steam coming out of her ears as she geared up for battle. "If I were you, I shouldn't count on it."

"Fie on you, lassie! 'Tis high time you were married with a wee bairn to bounce on your knee."

"Humph! If grandchildren are your aim, I suggest you scare up a younger candidate."

"Dinna confuse the earl with Methuselah—nor me neither," Angus said huffily. "Had I a mind to, I dinna think I'd have trouble fathering more bairns."

"Are you thinking of taking a second wife? Is that why you are so eager to marry me off?"

"Whisht. Niver have I heard such rubbish. All I want is to see you comfortably settled."

So would I, Papa, so would I. Marrying Summerfield was too high a price to pay, though. Price? Annabel's expression turned cynical.

"Tell me, Papa, how much did it cost you to buy me a title?"

"Och! Dinna take that tone wi' me, lass. You will do as you are bid when the time comes. Away wi' ye now before I take a stick to ye!"

Observing her father's frogish features purpling, Annabel decided that while temporary retreat was not a bad idea it did not mean she was resigned to marrying a man who made her skin crawl, earl or no!

The major gazed in awe at the mound of crumpled linen lying on the floor of his cousin's bedchamber. He scarcely knew what to make of the growing pile of ruined neckclothes Summerfield kept discarding. Clearly the earl was in a pelter, triggered, no doubt, by his failure to achieve perfection in the tying of his cravat.

By chance, their eyes met in the mirror Summerfield used to arrange his neckcloth in a style dubbed the mathematical. The earl waved him toward a chair which Justin gratefully took because his thigh was aching.

With a final twitch to his neckcloth, the earl turned away from the mirror. "So, what do you think of my handiwork, major?"

Justin arched an eyebrow. "Give over, Godfrey. After a decade in uniform, I'm hardly the arbiter of current fashion."

Summerfield stiffened at this blasphemy. Then, recovering his composure, ventured mildly, "Who can blame me for wishing to don my best bib and tucker to pay my addresses?"

"You actually intend to marry a Cit's daughter, do you?"

The earl gave an indolent shrug. "For years, I entertained hopes that Great-uncle Bertie would cock up his toes. Instead, the curst octogenarian seems determined to outlive me. Mind you, I'm by no means certain he'll leave me anything when he passes on. With my creditors hounding me, I feel a bird in hand is worth two in a bush. In short, I've no choice but to stay the course. Besides, the gel's lineage is unexceptional on her mother's side of the family. Her grandmama was the late Lady Winthrop."

"So your bride is not entirely ineligible."

"Exactly so. And while we are on the subject of my upcoming marriage, I trust the prospect of being usurped by a more direct heir is not too unsettling."

"Perish the thought!" Justin hastened to reassure his cousin. "Have all the brats you want, with my blessings. The last thing I covet is your earldom."

Summerfield snorted. "If so, you're one in a million."

Justin bristled. "Are you calling me a liar, cousin?"

"Softly, fire eater. I've no reason to doubt your sincerity."

"Damned right, you don't! For the record, I can't wait to rejoin my regiment."

"Just so. Tell me, Major, how much longer do you expect to be on convalescent leave?"

"The surgeon insists bones knit slowly, so I expect I must hobble about a bit longer. But to return to the fascinating subject of your upcoming nuptials, when do I get to meet your intended?"

Summerfield responded with a crack of laughter. "I know I'm regarded as something of a loose screw in some quarters. But acquit me of being so stupid as to introduce a handsome devil such as yourself to my heiress until after we're wed."

"Gammon! I do not poach on another man's preserves."

"I never said you did. Yet why tempt fate by introducing my heiress to a career officer a decade younger than myself? The weaker sex has been known to swoon at the sight of a soldier's scarlet coat."

"Really, Godfrey, all women are not uniform-mad. Have you so little faith in her character?"

"It's not a question of faith. I prefer to leave nothing to chance. The gel's definitely a looker. Prettily behaved, too."

"Your intended sounds almost too good to be true."

"To be sure, yesterday was my lucky day. Indeed, I can't wait to get my hands on the huge dowry her stingy father agreed to pay me. Just as I can hardly wait to bed her."

" 'Ware, cousin," Justin warned. "Tradesmen are notoriously strait-laced. I doubt her father would tolerate any um . . . anticipation of your wedding night."

"Very true! Nor for that matter would Miss Drummond." Summerfield sighed. "Pity that."

Drummond? The major's thoughts reeled. No, surely he was mistaken. His cousin's heiress couldn't be the girl of Justin's dreams. Fate would not be so cruel. Summerfield was not fit to touch the hem of her gown.

Justin asked the question in as cool a voice as he could. "Godfrey, does your intended have red hair?"

"Why yes, she does." The earl's bloodshot eyes narrowed. "How on earth would you know that?"

Ironically, Justin mused, his cousin's boast of deflowering a faceless heiress had not troubled him especially. But once the name Drummond was spoken, the entire world seemed to tilt. The injustice of the spirited titian beauty being despoiled by his wastrel cousin left a bitter taste in his mouth. The notion of Summerfield squandering her fortune did not sit well either.

But never mind that his innards were churning. And never mind that he was having the devil's own time resisting an urge to darken his cousin's daylights. The earl was eyeing him suspiciously. Justin decided he'd best answer his question.

"A mutual acquaintance introduced us. And you are right. She's a beauty."

With studied insouciance, the earl flicked off the lid of an enameled snuff box he held in his palm. "I did not realize you'd begun to go about in society. Where precisely did you meet Annabel?"

He'd be damned before he offered his congratulations, Justin raged inwardly. The realization he was powerless to stop the wedding from taking place tormented him as he watched Summerfield take a pinch of snuff and carry it to his nose. The act set in motion a sneezing frenzy that wracked the earl's skeletal frame. The episode might have seemed comical, had not Justin been beyond even dark humor.

"We met at some overcrowded function. I'm afraid I cannot remember which one," he lied without the slightest compunction. "When my game leg acts up, events tend to run together."

A ripple of sardonic satisfaction vaulted through him. Yesterday, when Boswell had escorted him to a hackney in Cornhill Street, Justin, ecstatic to learn that he and Miss Drummond had a mutual acquaintance, had shamelessly picked the solicitor's brain. Not only did Annabel Drummond play the stock market, she was good at it. However, knowing his cousin was predisposed to squander Annabel's fortune in gaming hells and brothels, he saw no reason to tattle on her.

The major gave a ghost of a smile. That he and the delectable Annabel Drummond had met at the Royal Exchange would remain a closely-guarded secret.

Five

Her back ramrod straight, Annabel sat on the wooden settle in the anteroom of her man of business's office. Her stormy gaze and the linen handkerchief she twisted in her hands were clear signs of her agitated state of mind.

Perched on a high stool, the clerk's gaze kept straying from the ledger he was hunched over, to steal sly peeks at her. Not that she blamed him, this being the second time in a fortnight she'd shown up at the Royal Exchange without an appointment.

Kenneth Boswell appeared in the open doorway. His serious mien lightened as he moved toward her. "My dear Miss Drummond, what a delightful surprise."

Annabel rose to her feet. "My apologies for the intrusion. A crisis has developed since we last spoke and I need advice."

"Another investment you wish to unload before it starts to lose money? Hmm?"

She gave a rueful smile. "Would that it were that simple."

"Nigel, Miss Drummond looks as if she could stand some coffee. So could I."

The clerk scrambled off the high stool. "I'll pop off to Lloyd's. Back in a jiffy."

"Allow me." Boswell tucked Annabel's hand in his arm and led her into his private office.

Conversation remained general until Nigel had
fetched hot coffee and withdrew. Annabel did not mind.
The short respite gave her a chance to put her jumbled
thoughts in order. But once she'd removed her gloves
and picked up the steaming mug of coffee poured out
by the solicitor, she was ready to tell her tale of woe to
what she hoped would be a sympathetic ear.

"Now then, what can I do for you this fine February
morning?"

Fine was not the word she'd pick to describe the day's
weather, thought Annabel. True, the sun was shining,
but the air held a touch of frost, which had prompted
her to dress warmly in a plum-colored habit of blended
wool and silk, trimmed round the bodice with swans-
down.

But why quibble over an adjective? She had more important matters to discuss. "My future happiness is in
peril. You must help me sort out this tangle."

"Happy to oblige. Suppose we begin by you telling
me what's put you in such a passion?"

"As you wish. Behind my back, my father has arranged my marriage to the Earl of Summerfield. I met
his lordship for the first time a fortnight ago and disliked him intensely. And that was before Papa had told
me of his plans!"

Boswell stared at her, dumbstruck.

"It is clear my news has shocked you," said Annabel.
"Imagine how *I* felt when told. The only way I got
through the dinner party was by telling myself I had
to tolerate the dissipated roue's obsequious behavior for
one evening and that afterward, I need never set eyes
on him again. Imagine my dismay when Papa dropped
his bombshell the following day."

"To be sure, Miss Drummond, your father should
have been more forthcoming. But pray do not be too

hasty. Your grandmama's fondest wish was that you marry a nobleman.''

Annabel glowered at the solicitor. "Grandmama may have had hopes in that direction, but I sincerely doubt she'd force me to wed a man old enough to be my father—nobleman or no!''

Boswell had the grace to look chagrined. "Certainly, such a union would not be her first choice. However, I cannot in good conscience be less than candid. Pray forgive my bluntness, but a young lady with a father in trade cannot afford to be *too* particular.''

Annabel flinched at this plain speaking, but made a quick recovery. "Say what you will, sir, you'll never convince me Grandmama would wish me to marry a fortune hunter.''

"Surely fortune hunter is coming too strong,'' Boswell admonished. "Angus Drummond is far too shrewd to be hoodwinked.''

"No one is infallible. In this instance, I am persuaded his judgment is flawed.''

"You may well be right. All I'm saying is it is folly to cast off such an eligible suitor on the basis of one dinner party.''

"It is not just the dinner party upon which I base my aversion. I allowed myself to be persuaded into driving with him in his curricle in Hyde Park during the fashionable hour.''

Annabel gave a small shudder. The liberties the earl had attempted to take in broad daylight still outraged her.

"And?'' Boswell prompted.

" 'Tis a good thing that I care nothing for the *ton's* good opinion. Summerfield treated me like a lightskirt.''

"Gammon! No doubt you misunderstood the earl's behavior, which I am persuaded did not cross the line of acceptable conduct in the eyes of the *ton*—given that you are betrothed to each other."

Annabel cast Boswell a disappointed look. Obviously, he was not the sympathetic ear she'd hoped for.

"How society regards Summerfield's conduct is not the issue. His behavior is not acceptable to *me*. And so I told him to his face the last time I set eyes on him."

"I collect you avoided him ever since. Correct?"

Expression wary, she nodded.

"My dear, Miss Drummond, is that wise? People do improve upon further acquaintance. Why not get to know him better? Then, if you really feel you will not suit, I daresay your father will not force you into a union you find distasteful."

Eyes flashing, cheeks stained a dusky rose, Annabel scoffed, "Much you know! Papa's fondest ambition is to hobnob with the swells. Much he cares if I'm miserable, so long as he can boast that his daughter's a countess."

The solicitor wagged his head from side to side. "I fear my advice has fallen on deaf ears."

Annabel regarded him with raised eyebrows. "I hardly think so. I've yet to broach the subject I need advice on."

"Indeed," Boswell said dryly. "In that case, I must beg you to come directly to the point."

"Certainly. I know Grandmama willed me the town house in Russell Square. I wish to know if I have the right to sell it."

Alarm etched his austere countenance. "Sell it? Have you gone queer in the attic?"

Annabel glared at the solicitor. "Sir, I am not a child. If you wish to continue to handle my affairs I suggest you cease to patronize me and address my concerns."

His expression harried, Boswell hastened to mend his fences. "I did not mean to give offense. But to suggest selling such a valuable property. . . . Naturally, I was taken aback."

"Just so. At the risk of shocking you further, I beg leave to tell you I do not wish to marry anyone—much less the detestable nobleman foisted upon me by my socially ambitious father. I am well aware at four-and-twenty I need not obey him. But knowing Papa, he'll make my life a misery should I openly oppose him. Thus I must devise a counter plan. Do I make myself clear so far, Mr. Boswell?"

"Of a certainty. Though to be honest, your resolve to remain a spinster troubles me. A woman is fulfilled through marriage. Surely you want children?"

His demeanor was so earnest Annabel almost forgave him for his presumption. "Sir, it is unlikely we will see eye-to-eye on the subject of matrimony. Of course I want children, but I feel the loss of my independence is too high a price to pay. Seven years ago, I dared not tell Grandmama my true feelings, but I was not sorry her illness prevented my comeout. I did not wish to be paraded like a prized mare on the marriage mart. I have not changed my mind in the interim. The truth is I do not wish to be subjugated by a male of the species."

Eyes round as coach wheels, Boswell observed, "That is certainly an . . . um original view."

"It is simply how I feel. Now then, to the crux of the matter. If I may sell the town house, I plan to set up my own household with the proceeds. So tell me, sir, do I or do I not have the right to sell the house Grandmama left me?"

His pinched features weighed down with sorrow, Boswell slowly shook his head. "At present you do not. Not without the consent of the three trustees Lady Winthrop appointed to guard your interests."

A sudden chill prompted Annabel to wrap her fingers round the stoneware mug, seeking warmth from the hot liquid it contained. "I suppose it would do no harm to speak to each of them personally. Perhaps I can persuade them to allow it."

Boswell snorted. "If I were you, I shouldn't count on it. All three are staunch Tories set in their ways. Your plan to set up your own establishment is bound to shock them."

Hopes dashed, she rose with dignity and slowly drew on her gloves. "I thank you for your time, sir."

Her hand was reaching for the doorknob when Boswell called, "Wait!"

Turning to face him, she said, "Yes?"

"I would be derelict in my duty did I not inform you that in another year the trusteeship ends and you may dispose of the property as you see fit."

Annabel's eyes widened. "Are you saying that once I am five-and-twenty, I may do as I please with the house?"

"Exactly so."

She gave a throaty chuckle. "I really cannot see myself managing to stall both Papa and Lord Summerfield for an entire year, can you?"

"Indeed not." He awarded her a tight smile. "However, given your aversion to matrimony, I imagine you will leave no stone unturned."

Spirits deflated, eyes downcast, Annabel glided along the Royal Exchange's paved walkway toward Threadneedle Street. Bringing order to her roiling emotions appeared futile. Frustrated, she quickened her pace—only to run smack into a broad, manly chest, made all the more splendid by the scarlet uniform that adorned it.

Thrown off balance, Annabel might have toppled but

for the strong sinewy arm that gripped hers above the elbow to steady her.

"Well curl my liver! If it isn't the redoubtable Miss Drummond, intent upon causing me another pratfall."

"No such thing!" Annabel protested once recognition dawned. "Unhand me, Major!"

Justin gave a throaty chuckle. "Not so fast, sweetheart. While it is true I've traded in my crutches for a cane, I'm by no means as steady on my pins as I'd like. Before I release you, I require your solemn word that you've no plans to knock me down."

Annabel glared at him. On the outs with *all* men in general, the last thing she wanted to do was reassure one. Yet she did owe him an apology.

"Upon my word, I've no such intention. Last time was an accident."

Ducking his head, he eyed her skeptically. "Truly?"

Annabel's heart raced. Their heads were almost touching. His warm breath stirred emotions she would just as soon remained dormant, particularly now when she was still upset with her solicitor's lack of empathy.

"Yes, truly," she whispered.

His light blue eyes held such tenderness Annabel thought he might kiss her, and she couldn't help but wonder how his generously full lips would feel pressed against hers. Then, he simultaneously straightened and eased his grip on her arm. Oddly disappointed, she pulled her arm free and began to massage the spot where his fingers had just been.

He cast her a concerned look. "Did I hurt you?"

Annabel flushed. Of course he hadn't. It was simply that his touch had aroused peculiar sensations . . . longings she had no name for and had no intention of owning up to. Yet once they were no longer touching, she felt a sense of loss.

"Did I?" he persisted.

Annabel shook her head. "I'm not so fragile as all that. I owe you a belated apology for knocking you down when you were on crutches. At the time the incident occurred, you were spirited off before I had a chance to do so."

Justin's features relaxed in a rakish smile. "If you truly wish to make amends, the slate will be wiped clean, provided you allow me to treat you to a cup of coffee at Lloyd's."

"What you suggest is impossible. We haven't been formally introduced."

"Ah, but we have! By our mutual man of business, Kenneth Boswell."

"Why, of course. How stupid of me not to remember!"

"Now that you have, what do you say to a cup of coffee?"

Though tempted, Annabel shook her head. "I fear I'm not the best company today. The reason I wasn't looking where I was going is that I'm vexed with Boswell, who treats me as if I had no more judgment than a babe in arms."

"Does he? Why the insensitive cad!" Justin responded, tongue-in-cheek.

"Just so. Now if you'll excuse me, Major, I must go."

Regret replaced amusement in his light blue eyes. "Must you, truly? Surely you have time for a cup of coffee."

"I fear not. My coachman has been circling the exchange for ages. If I don't join him at once, he's sure to raise an alarm."

Justin looked as if he were all set to argue further, but apparently he changed his mind at the last minute because he said, "In that case, allow me to escort you to your meeting spot."

After handing Annabel into her carriage, Justin

watched it pull into the brisk traffic so prevalent on a weekday in London's financial district. He watched until the carriage entered the curve that led into Poultry Street. He watched until it passed out of sight, before he turned and reentered the courtyard of the Royal Exchange.

As he headed toward Boswell's office, his step was no longer as jaunty as it'd been before Annabel Drummond had literally run into him. Suddenly weary, he leaned more heavily on his cane and wondered if he were overdoing things. The last thing he needed was another setback that would prevent him from rejoining his regiment at the earliest possible date.

His thoughts returned to the lovely Annabel. Had he persisted a bit longer, he was all but certain he'd have changed her mind and she'd have come with him for coffee. Yet, considering his presently limited prospects, his invitation had been downright foolish. After all, what did he have to offer an heiress about to wed an earl? To be sure, Wellington had mentioned him a time or two in the dispatches, but a career officer's pay only stretched so far. At the moment, he couldn't afford a wife. And, of course, he had too much respect for Annabel to offer her anything less than marriage.

Inside the carriage bound for Russell Square, Annabel was still of two minds in regard to Major Camden's invitation to join him for coffee. Closing her eyes, she envisioned herself seated across from him in a booth at Lloyd's and found herself wishing that she'd been bold enough to accept his invitation. For a fleeting second, she'd believed that in him she'd found the sympathetic ear she craved so badly. But of course that was wishful thinking on her part, was it not?

Pull yourself together! Annabel admonished as the car-

riage drew up to the mews behind her town house.
True, Major Camden was as handsome as he could
stare, but what had that to say to anything!

Several miles east of the Royal Exchange, in a garret
with a view of the London Docks, Angus sat at a gateleg
table that had seen better days. At his right shoulder
stood his solicitor, come to bear witness to the delicate
transaction about to take place. The Earl of Summerfield occupied the cluttered room's only other chair.
With him was his private secretary, a mousy looking
specimen, growing a little grayer and little more wiz-
ened each year he served the Camden family.

Arranged in neat stacks on the table's scratched surface were bank drafts in the amount of four thousand
guineas and two copies of the settlement about to be
signed before witnesses by the consenting parties. Pre-
dictably, the earl noted only the bank drafts. Indeed,
the money was his sole incentive for rising at this ungodly hour and traveling crosstown to the smelly London Docks.

"Och, mon. I dinna have a whole day ta waste. Have
ye read the agreement?"

"I have. I'm ready to sign if you are."

"That I am, my fine laird, that I am."

Angus called for ink and quill pens. Minutes after
the deed was done, he dismissed his dour-faced solicitor
with a curt nod. Before their respective signatures had
completely dried, Summerfield's private secretary
stepped forward and gathered the bank drafts into a
valise brought along for that purpose.

To Angus, watching his hard-earned blunt rapidly
disappear was a gut-wrenching experience. He started
to turn away, but his flight from reality was stymied by
Summerfield's hand on his shoulder.

"Tell your lovely daughter I shall call on her tomorrow afternoon to take her for a drive in Hyde Park."

Angus shrugged off the unwanted restraint. "I'll tell her. But the lass has a mind of her own."

The earl arched an eyebrow. "Are you suggesting she means to continue to defy me now that the wedding contract has been signed?"

"Who ken sae wat a female will take a notion ta do?"

Summerfield shot him a stern look. "You are the minx's father. Surely, she'll obey you. See that she's ready at two o'clock sharp."

With that, he spun on his heel and strode from the room. In his wake trudged his private secretary. Once alone, Angus sobered. He did not relish the fireworks he was liable to encounter when he delivered the earl's message to Annabel.

Stubborn lass, he groused. Why couldn't she have inherited her mother's biddable nature instead of his contentiousness? A reluctant grin surfaced. Och, he'd known the bonny lass would ever be a handful the day she was born. One peek into her cradle had revealed those fiery red curls that framed her wee face. In his salad days, Angus reflected, his own thatch had been the same shade as Annabel's. Now it was more of a drab orange with the exception of graying temples that matched his mutton chop whiskers.

He released a deep sigh. Any more scenes like the one he'd endured a fortnight ago, and his hair would go completely gray in no time. Annabel had behaved like a spoiled brat. Instead of thanking him prettily for arranging such a splendid match, she'd waxed defiant.

But surely, Angus reasoned, she'd come round once she had time to grow used to the idea of her upcoming marriage. Notwithstanding having just parted with four thousand pounds, he began to feel less downpin. He'd done right by his daughter, and surely one day the lass would thank him for his gude sense. Would she not?

Preoccupied, Angus was for the most part oblivious to the horns, whistles and bells that accompanied Thames traffic, as well as the curses of the burly laborers loading cargo onto his flag ship. Nor did the reek of fish or rotting garbage cause more than a ripple of awareness. Countless years spent in his tiny garret office had inured him to the stench.

His ruminations came to a jarring halt when Colin McPherson entered the garret, breathing fire. "Angus, have ye run mad? What do you mean by this note you sent round to Lloyd's?"

The Scotsman's frogish features instantly assumed an air of innocence. "Kin ye not read, mon?"

"Of course I can. But I dinna believe you'd do something so corkbrained as to not insure four ships about to set sail for the Orient."

"Dinna try to dissuade me. I've made up my mind."

"Are ye daft? What if one is lost at sea?"

Icy prickles of fear needled the back of Angus's neck as possible consequences of his rash decision flashed before his eyes. Nevertheless, having just parted with four thousand pounds, he was in no mood to part with any more of his blunt. Not after he'd paid for years through the nose for insurance with only minor losses he could easily absorb himself. So, mind set in stone, he geared up for battle.

"Aye, 'tis a wee risk, but one I'm willing to take. So cease your nattering."

McPherson snorted. "Without insurance, yer liable for the cargo and obliged to pay the merchants involved out of yer own pocket. Ye could go bankrupt. Ye could even end up in debtor's prison."

"Och, Colin, dinna fash yourself. To be sure, 'tis a risk but the odds are in my favor."

McPherson had blustered into the garret bristling with confidence. But now, in the face of such implacable intransigence, he seemed to deflate before his associate's protuberant eyes.

"Are ye certain, Angus?"

"Aye. Dinna sulk, mon. One lost commission won't ruin ye."

"Commission be damned! The risk is too great. Dinna do this."

"Whisht! Away wi' ye now, I've work ta do and your gloomy phiz is putting me off."

McPherson yanked open the door then struck a dramatic pose. "Weel, mon, niver say I dinna warn ye!"

Six

Annabel's midnight blue eyes shimmered with unspilt tears as they swept the room she'd considered her private retreat for the past seven years. It grieved her to leave the tranquil setting but her social-climbing parent left her no other choice. Either she stole away like a thief in the night or in three days she'd find herself wed to the odious Earl of Summerfield.

Her gaze had almost come full circle when she espied her silver-backed mirror, brush, and comb lying on the dressing table. With a cry of dismay, she scooped them off the marble surface and stuffed them into her already-bulging bandbox. Her hand covered her thumping heart. What a close call! The matched set had been a gift from Grandmama. Annabel would never forgive herself if she'd left it behind.

Annabel frowned. Four months ago, she'd have given odds the wedding she dreaded would never take place. Even when Boswell told her she could not sell the town house for another year, she'd refused to be daunted. She'd promptly explored other avenues. To her sorrow, so far nothing she'd tried had worked.

Her upper teeth rested lightly on her lower lip. She'd thought of taking refuge with the McPhersons, but decided she was much too fond of the couple to subject them to her father's volatile temper when crossed. She'd sought work as a domestic servant, only to be stymied by her lack of credible references. But a far worse set-back occurred when the proprietor of the domestic agency tattled on her. Papa had been so furious, he'd threatened to starve her into submission.

An idle threat, of course. For all his bluster, Annabel knew he was fond of her. Which wasn't to say he was willing to let her small rebellion go unpunished. After venting his spleen, he'd confined her to her room for a sennight. Nor was that the end of it. After dining off dinner trays for a week, she'd emerged to find he'd hired two burly bodyguards to shadow her every step. Used to coming and going as she pleased, their constant surveillance whittled away at her self esteem. That she was not even allowed to visit her dressmaker in the Strand unless accompanied by her embarrassing escort, infuriated her. But the final straw proved to be the sole exception to Papa's edict.

Only if accompanied by her fiance could she rid herself of her body guards. Which, since the last person on earth she desired to be with was Summerfield, didn't suit her at all.

Annabel's chin wobbled. Countless times in the last four months she'd begged her father to reconsider his mad-brained scheme to make her a countess. Nothing she'd said had changed his mind. Pigheaded to a fault, he truly thought he knew what was best for her. She was to be a June bride, like it or no!

Not even when she'd overcome her maidenly reserve to confess that she couldn't bear the earl's touch did Papa relent. To her bitter disappointment, he'd dismissed her revulsion as bridal nerves.

Far below, the longcase clock chimed five times. Startled, she realized she must not linger, else she'd miss her chance to elude her bodyguards. She tied on her rolled-rim straw bonnet. Eying it in the looking glass, she conceded it looked rather forlorn without its trimming. Yet she wished to travel incognito and ostentatious display could defeat her purpose. Bonnet strings tied, she glanced at her bottle green gown from which she'd stripped every scrap of lace edging its hem and sleeve cuffs.

Dark smudges underlined her eyes. She couldn't remember the last time she'd gotten a decent night's sleep. From the day Papa told her she was to marry the odious Earl of Summerfield, what little rest she got came in random snatches, which all too often left her temporarily groggy.

Turning away from the mirror, she draped a Kashmir shawl over one arm and picked up her bandbox. She deplored the necessity of the step she was about to take. Yet she certainly did not wish to marry Summerfield. Her only alternative was to go to ground in Sussex until her twenty-fifth birthday passed. Only then, she reasoned with an unrepentant grin, could she hope to gain the upper hand.

The sky had just begun to pinken with the upcoming dawn when Annabel let herself out the front door of the Georgian house overlooking Russell Square. As she set off toward Hart Street, where she hoped to find a hackney hovering near Bloomsbury Market, her grin widened as she imagined Papa's amazement when she sold the town house right out from under him.

Annabel leaned back against the squabs as the hackney trundled past the Bank of England. Being abroad so early, she'd had trouble finding a cab. Once underway, there was little street traffic to impede their progress, so it took less than an hour to travel from Bloomsbury to the city.

The hackney drew to a halt at the Threadneedle Street entrance of the Royal Exchange. Alighting,

Annabel paid off the driver and glided across the deserted courtyard. She came to an abrupt stop in front of Kenneth Boswell's office. She jiggled the knob. Locked of course. Her expression mirrored keen disappointment.

"Slug-a-bed," she muttered.

She firmly swallowed her irritation. It was barely seven. None of the other offices or shops had flung open their doors either. The business world was not subject to her whims. Because she had a stage to catch was no reason to expect her solicitor to be on the job before regular business hours.

Yet she could not wait indefinitely for him to show up. Indeed, she was in a quandary. The last Brighton bound coach left at a quarter to nine on the dot. If she missed it, she must wait another day, and who knew what new restrictions tomorrow would bring? She must be aboard The Comet today as it crossed London Bridge.

Too restless to stand still, she embarked on a brisk stroll beneath the arcade formed by Roman arches. Whatever was she going to do? True, the stagecoach office was only a few blocks away. If she couldn't find a cab, she'd have to walk. The latest she could leave the Exchange was eight o'clock, allowing herself forty-five minutes to reach the yard, buy her ticket, and board.

On the other hand, for the next year she must make do with the profits from her investments. Thus, it was imperative that she stay in touch with her man of business. Accessibility was the chief reason she'd picked Tunbridge Wells as her hideaway. Situated less than twenty miles from the heart of London's financial district, the resort town had the added advantage of no longer being in fashion. This narrowed the chances of her rubbing shoulders with one of Summerfield's cronies, who might decide to tip him off.

Annabel climbed the curved stairs to the upper level on the off chance that Boswell might be drinking coffee at Lloyd's Coffee House. However, her momentarily raised hopes plummeted after a thorough inspection of the premises. Ironically, Kenneth Boswell excepted, all the world and his brother seemed to be sipping coffee.

Annabel wound up back at Boswell's locked office, where she consulted the ladies' watch pinned to her bodice. She had only fifteen minutes to spare before she must leave. Nothing for it! she decided. She must write Boswell a note giving her direction and slip it beneath his door before making her way to the Spread Eagle in Gracechurch Street.

It was just after nine o'clock in the morning. Angus generally arrived at the London Docks a bit later, but today he'd been too restless to linger over breakfast and had slipped out of the town house with no one the wiser. He emitted a heavy sigh. Truth be told, he came away early to avoid being badgered by Annabel, who was no more resigned to being wed now than she'd been in February, when first informed of the marriage he'd contracted.

Frustrated, he shook his fist at the ceiling of the swaying town coach. By God, he'd let Annabel stall long enough. June was the best time for a wedding and he intended to see his daughter a countess before the month was out. Furthermore, after investing four thousand pounds in her future, he had every right to expect her to cooperate. Especially as, three days hence, he'd be expected to shell out the second installment right after the ceremony.

Blue-deviled, Angus trudged up the rickety staircase

and entered the dockside garret he rented by the year for a pittance. He threw open a window, then wrinkled his nose in disdain of the myriad of noxious scents that rushed into the stuffy loft along with the change of air. Peering out, his barrel chest swelled with pride as he gazed down at two merchant ships taking on cargo. He owned both. They were bound for the Caribbean on the evening tide. Any minute now he expected McPherson to show up to badger him to buy insurance. Today he'd oblige him. It was too nerve wracking not to.

Still, at present his liquid assets were at low ebb. When he delivered the second installment to Summerfield right after the ceremony, he'd scarcely have tuppence left.

No question, thought Angus, he'd feel immeasurably better about such a large outlay once the four merchant ships he'd neglected to insure in February sailed into the harbor. He'd looked for their return in May. Here it was mid-June and still no sign of them. Not that he was unduly worried. Storms often blew ships off course. All the same he'd be glad when they finally made port.

A heavy footfall on the rickety stairs claimed his attention. In response to a firm rap on the far side of the flimsy door, Angus barked, "Come on in, Colin."

Huffing and puffing, a red-faced McPherson burst into the garret. He barred the door and said, "Brace yourself, mon. I've terrible tidings."

"Weel, dinna stand there like a carving from Madame Tussaud's wax works. Open yer budget!"

"Lloyd's is abuzz with the news. All four of yer ships sank off the Cape of Good Hope."

His complexion the color of oatmeal, Angus gripped the window sill with both hands so hard his knuckles turned white. " 'Tis a disaster," he croaked, gazing unseeingly down at the cobblestone street beneath the garret window.

"Aye. Once the merchants with cargo aboard find out ye dinna insure the ships, they'll keelhaul ye. Best shab off at once!"

"Gude advice. Would that I could heed it. As things stand I'm skating close to bankruptcy. All is lost if I dinna see my two remaining ships out of the harbor before the rabble think to impound them."

"With or withoot insurance?"

Angus gave a rusty chuckle. "With of course. Do I survive this crisis, niver agin will I take such a foolish chance."

"Weel, in that case, begone with ye! I'll see both set sail whilst ye run for cover."

Instead of agreeing, Angus exclaimed, "The mob is already gatherin'. Pounds to pigeons, they're oot to wring my neck."

" 'Tis hard to believe. Mind if I have a look?"

His complexion a shade grayer, Angus stepped aside. McPherson peered out the open window at the crowd of irate merchants below. The unruly mob already claimed most of the narrow street. But what caught his attention was the lone figure seemingly oblivious to the melee, who steadily approached the ramshackle structure that housed Drummond's dockside office.

"It seems Kenneth Boswell is aboot to pay you a call."

"Who?" Angus asked.

"Ye dinna ken his name but ye may have seen him at Lloyd's. He's a solicitor who rents an office at the Royal Exchange."

"All weel and gude, but what can he want of me?"

Boswell's vigorous rap on the flimsy door sent Angus scurrying to open it before it came off its hinges. Expression dour, he motioned him inside.

"Angus Drummond, I presume? My name is—"

"Kenneth Boswell. McPherson tells me you're a solicitor."

"I am. You must wonder why I've come."

"Aye. State yer business."

The solicitor cast McPherson an uneasy glance before addressing Angus. "No offense, but it might be best if I spoke to you in private."

"Och, dinna mind Colin. I'd trust him wi' my own datter."

"I see. By coincidence, it is in regard to Miss Drummond that I have come."

"This regards Annabel?"

Boswell nodded. "Ordinarily I wouldn't dream of betraying a confidence. However, I cannot in good conscience allow Miss Drummond to travel on a public coach and take up residence in Tunbridge Wells. To behave in such a helter skelter fashion could ruin her reputation."

"Och! Niver say Annabel is running away?"

"I fear so."

Angus looked thunderstruck. While he recovered his voice, McPherson took over. "How come ye ken the lassie's plans?"

"Because I'm her man of business. I served the late Lady Winthrop in the same capacity. She recommended me to her granddaughter."

Angus looked so fierce that Boswell took an involuntary step backward. "Man of Business? Ha! Monkey business more like?"

"On the contrary. She has a modest sum invested in consols and owns a respectable portfolio of stocks. On occasion, she takes a flyer in commodities. Her investments require constant diligence and frequent consultation between us. No doubt that is why she dropped off a note giving me her new direction at my office on her way to the Spread Eagle yard. It would never have done to leave London without telling me where she was bound, would it now?"

Ashen-faced, Angus sank onto the rickety chair behind the gateleg table. He took several deep breaths before he was able to continue.

"So Annabel plays the market, does she? And makes a profit more often than not, right?"

Boswell nodded. "For a mere female of modest means, she's had remarkable success. She has an uncanny knack for knowing what to buy and when. And even more important, when she should cut her losses. Even Rothschild respects her judgment."

Angus awarded Boswell's bemused recital a rusty chuckle. He turned to McPherson. "Hear that Colin, the bonny lass is as shrewd as they come."

McPherson nodded. "A chip off the old block to be sure. But what do ye propose to do? Will you call off the wedding or go after her?"

"I dinna ken. I need a wee bit o' time to mull things over."

With that, Angus lapsed into a pensive silence. The harsh truth stared him in the face. By letting social ambition overrule all else, he'd managed to alienate his own daughter. Rather than marry the bridegroom Angus had chosen, Annabel preferred to take her chances in a hostile world.

Deep in thought, he wandered over to the open window and gazed down at the angry melee in the narrow street below. Much as he deplored her defection, he secretly admired her pluck. His fondness for the bonny lass was such that he seriously considered letting her go free.

After all, he reasoned, having bungled his own financial affairs so badly, what right had he to impose his will on his daughter? Obviously, she had a shrewd head on her shoulders. Having to watch a dissolute husband waste the ready would pain her.

An angry shout from the milling crowd beneath the

garret window brought his own business crisis back into focus. The mob was out for his blood. He'd be lucky if he escaped their vengeance with his whole skin. Canceling the wedding would be a bad mistake, Angus decided. As the Countess of Summerfield, Annabel would be insulated from the scandal sure to ensue once his dubious business practices were publicly aired.

A decidedly agitated Boswell interrupted the dour Scotsman's ruminations. "Sir, every minute counts. I went to the Spread Eagle yard first. I'd hoped to intercept her in order to avoid betraying a confidence. The Comet embarked for Brighton an hour ago with Miss Drummond aboard. If you delay pursuit until she reaches Tunbridge Wells, finding her will be tantamount to finding a needle in a haystack."

Angus regarded the solicitor with such marked incredulity that beads of perspiration dotted the latter's prominent forehead. "I dinna ken. You said the lass left you a note."

Boswell wiped the sweat from his brow with a snowy white handkerchief. "The note does not give her exact address. I'm to write her in care of the local vicar."

"Annabel will doubtless take umbrage at your meddling."

Boswell visibly stiffened. "I don't make a habit of it. But I could hardly permit Miss Drummond to set forth with not even a chaperone to lend her countenance."

Angus stared at him for a full minute, then sneered, "You, sir, are a stiff-necked ignoramus. Rest assured the minute I catch up with Annabel, I weel recommend she dismiss you and hire a mon of honor to handle her affairs."

Seven

Major Justin Camden gazed about the dining room of the Earl of Summerfield's town house in Little Brook Street. For years, Justin reflected, the titular head of the Camden family had leased out the drafty mausoleum and lived in rented digs in South Audley, more suited to the needs of a carefree bachelor on the town. But his upcoming nuptials had obliged the earl to take up residence.

"How is it?" asked Summerfield.

Justin lifted his goblet abrim with port wine. His nostrils flared as he breathed in its heady aroma. Venturing a sip, he rolled the wine around his tongue, savoring its sweetness before he finally swallowed.

"Excellent body, rich taste." He kissed his fingers. "Nectar for the gods."

The earl gave a braying laugh. "Doing it up too brown, cousin. No need to wax poetic."

Grinning, Justin absent-mindedly rubbed his thigh. In late March more shrapnel had surfaced and been dug out by the surgeon. The wound had healed rapidly. Justin could now walk with scarcely a limp, and need only rely on his cane when he overdid things a trifle.

"Leg giving you trouble?"

He shrugged. "Nothing I can't handle. Stiffens up if I sit too long in one spot."

Summerfield's face was flushed from frequent imbibing during the long drawn-out meal. However, this was something of a farewell dinner, so if his host was a trifle bosky there was ample excuse. Besides, Justin himself was a trifle castaway so in no position to cast stones.

Replete from their tasty midnight supper, they'd agreed to split a bottle of port. Slated to set sail for Portugal in a few days' time, Justin preferred to bask in the wine-induced mellow glow while it lasted. Things would be grim enough once he rejoined his regiment.

Summerfield rubbed his palms together, a look of avid relish in his bloodshot eyes. "Think of it, Major. Three days hence, I shall sup with my fiery-haired bride."

Justin's jaw went rigid and the mouthful of wine he'd just taken suddenly tasted like vinegar.

Think of it? Ha! It would please him never to think of it! The image of his dissolute cousin bedding the titian beauty turned his stomach.

"Just so, cousin."

He manfully swallowed his bile and forced his clenched fists to relax. When Summerfield continued prosing, Justin chose to ignore his idle boasts of his sexual prowess. Better that, he conceded sardonically, than give in to an ardent urge to tap his smug cousin's claret.

He silently cursed the earl for broaching the subject. Yet he couldn't seem to stop himself from dwelling on it. The unsavory image of that sweet, unsullied virgin being bedded by this insensitive braggart refused to be banished.

He quelled a sigh. It was the way of the world. Nothing he could say or do would prevent such an abomination from taking place. Besides, he reminded himself for the umpteenth time, even if Annabel Drummond were not promised to his cousin, even if Justin had met her under different circumstances, his present lack of prospects would prevent him from courting her. Indeed, had a maiden aunt not left him a small legacy,

he'd never have been able to scrape up enough rhino
to buy himself a commission in the Light Infantry.

He squared his shoulders. A man of honor drew the
line at persuading a beautiful heiress to follow the drum.

"My lord?"

Justin eyed the wraith-like figure of his cousin's valet,
who'd somehow managed the seemingly impossible feat
of being leaner and bonier than his master.

"What the devil do you want, Danvers?" demanded
the earl.

"Your lordship has a caller."

Summerfield cast him an incredulous look. "At this
time of night?"

"A Mr. Drummond, your lordship. I told him you
were engaged but he insists it's important."

The earl beamed. "So Angus has come calling, has
he? Well, don't stand there like a block, Danvers. Show
the man in."

As the valet backed from the room, Summerfield said
in an urgent undertone. "Guard you tongue, Major.
Drummond's a slippery cove."

The invective did not strike Justin as an appropriate
way to refer to one's future father-in-law, but then he
was just an innocent bystander. Ponderous footfalls grew
steadily louder until a short, sturdy figure trudged into
the room. The Scotsman possessed a lantern jaw miti-
gated by muttonchop whiskers, and a thatch of orange
hair shot with silver at the temples. His frock coat,
though well brushed, looked so bedraggled Justin wondered if he'd slept in it. Justin's nose twitched as he
caught a distinct whiff of something that bore a distinct
affinity to rotten eggs wafting his way from the earl's
midnight caller.

So this was Annabel's father, he thought. After inten-

sive perusal, Justin decided that while Drummond's
navy blue eyes evinced shrewd intelligence, he was in
dire want of a bath, a valet and possibly a new tailor.
Judging by the entrenched lines in his face, his dour
demeanor appeared ingrained. What Justin found most
troubling was the grayish tinge to his complexion, which
made the Scotsman look as if he were sickening from
some unnamed malady.

"Greetings, Drummond. Can I pour you a glass of
port?"

Angus shook his head. He suffered from a sour stomach and dare not chance it. The constant jarring his
innards had received during his hot pursuit of his wayward daughter had left him with a bad case of dyspepsia.

"Pity. It is an excellent vintage. But I am forgetting
my manners. Allow me to present my second cousin
once removed, Major Justin Camden."

"Pleased ta met ye."

The major started to rise, but Drummond quickly
urged, "Nae, kept your seat, Camden. I dinna mean ta
barge in on your dinner."

So Justin contented himself with a nod and a warm
smile. He stared in silent bemusement at what he suspected were tomato seeds and bits of egg yolk embedded in Drummond's gray whiskers.

"Father of the bride, right?" he ventured.

"Aye, that I am, sur."

Looking worn to a frazzle, Angus addressed the earl.
"I must needs speak to ye in private."

"My dear fellow, whatever you have to say to me may
be said in front of my cousin. I'm not big on secrets."

Drummond's undershot jaw jutted further forward,
creating a striking resemblance to a stubborn frog determined to have its way. Stifling a laugh, Justin rose
as gracefully as he could manage, given a stiff leg
caused by sitting long enough to cramp.

"Godfrey, I need to walk out the kink in my bum leg. I'll take a stroll on the terrace and perhaps blow a cloud whilst you two put your heads together."

Drummond cast him a suspicious look, then apparently satisfied by what he read in Justin's face, relented. "I'm obliged to ye, Major."

Justin tried not to limp too badly as he made good his exit.

Once alone, the earl gazed at his future father-in-law and said, "Now then, Drummond, why are you here?"

Angus opened his mouth but no words came out. Only a croak.

Summerfield gave a mirthless chuckle. "Speechless for once? Shall I guess then? Perchance has my shy bride decided to cry off?"

Angus shook his head so vigorously, it was a wonder it didn't roll off. Of course, Annabel dinna wish to marry the earl. She never had. But it was imperative that he put a good face on things.

"Och! Mere wedding jitters. Naught to signify."

"Well if Annabel is not the problem, I cannot begin to guess what brings you. Pray enlighten me."

Angus began to sweat. Much as he'd prefer to keep mum about his current financial tangle, it was simply not possible. He faced financial ruin and could end up in debtor's prison. At all costs, he must prevent his only daughter from being tarred with the same brush. And the only way to insure this did not happen was to see her safely wed to the earl.

Summerfield's flushed countenance darkened to a purplish red. A sure sign his patience was wearing thin.

"Look here, despite the ungodly hour, I granted you an audience. So either open your budget or begone!"

Angus would rather swallow live worms than come

with hat in hand to beg a favor, but had no other recourse. Annabel's future was at stake.

"I expected my flagship and three others to return from the Orient long since. But they hae no reached Lunnon yet."

Nor would they ever, thought Angus. But he dare not tell Summerfield the truth. At all costs, he must be kept in the dark until after the wedding.

The earl eyed him cynically. "Do my ears deceive me? Or are you hinting you don't have the four thousand guineas due me immediately after the ceremony?"

Angus's shoulders slumped. "I need a wee more time ta gather it together."

Summerfield lifted both eyebrows. "You've had four months."

Angus toyed briefly with the idea of admitting he'd amassed the entire four thousand pounds but that McPherson had had to use most of it to placate Angus's outraged creditors and to bribe the dockmaster and his minions. Ah well, at least his remaining two ships had sailed on the evening tide. When he'd dragged Annabel back to Russell Square, he'd found McPherson waiting to tell him so.

But Summerfield expected a response to his latest sally. Sweating profusely, Angus cast his eyes heavenward and prayed for absolution for the whisker he was about to tell.

"I hae one thousand guineas on hand and weel make up the difference the minute my four overdue merchant ships dock."

The earl's pale blue eyes glittered with malice. "Either cough up all four thousand pounds before the ceremony or the wedding's off."

Summerfield stood with his arms folded across his narrow chest and his jawbone locked in a rigid line. All in all an impregnable fortress to lay siege to, Angus admitted. Nevertheless, being a scrapper who'd built his merchant fleet from next to nothing, it was not in his character to accept defeat without one hell of a fight.

"Ye can no do that. We've a signed contract."

"Contract be dammed! I refuse to be gulled."

Angus stared at the earl's stringy neck, wondering if he had enough strength in his hands to wring it. Probably not, he decided glumly. Especially not on a day like this—a day chock-full of ill tidings that had sapped his stamina. He sighed inwardly. It was bad enough to learn he'd lost the bulk of his fleet. Being pelted with garbage by angry creditors as he'd fled the docks was an humiliation he was unlikely to forget in a hurry.

The June air held the pleasant aroma of honeysuckle as Justin ground the butt of his cigarette under the heel of his boot. He'd long since worked out the kinks in his leg and was now eager to rejoin his cousin. Exercising caution, he eased the terrace door ajar just in time to catch the tail end of the combatants' conversation.

"Dinna be an ass. I'll make up the difference. All I need is a wee bit more time."

"Bloody skinflint! Pay up or suffer the consequences."

"Dinna even think of leaving the bonny lass at the altar," Drummond warned heatedly. "Should ye be so daft, I'll sue for breach of promise."

"Go straight to the devil!" Summerfield invited. "No court in the land will side with you."

Justin couldn't decide whether the honorable thing to do was to retreat and let the two foes thrash things out, or whether he ought to interfere before one of the combatants did in the other. Peering through the crack between the terrace door and the door jamb, he was just in time to witness Drummond's swan song.

Looking more than ever like a disgruntled frog, Angus croaked, "Dinna think to intimidate me. If ye dinna show up at St. George's on Monday next, I'll sue ye fer damages."

With that, the Scotsman spun on his heel and stalked from the room in high dudgeon. As his footfalls faded, Justin widened the terrace door and stepped into the dining room. His cousin sat huddled in his chair at the head of the table, his thin frame shaking with anger.

"By God, that knave deserves to be taught a lesson!" he exclaimed once he noted Justin's presence.

"I could not help overhearing the last few angry exchanges. What do you plan to do?"

The earl gave a bitter laugh. "Never one to mince words, are you, Major? As to whether I'll be so gauche as to leave my intended waiting at the altar, I've no idea. Nor will I know the answer to that until I've rooted out my solicitor and ordered him to put his ear to the ground. I need to know what prompted Angus's midnight call. Normally, he's too canny to expose his hand. Depend upon it, there's more to this than meets the eye. So before I make up my mind one way or the other, I need more information."

Justin digested this then ventured cautiously, "Much as I hate to take the wind from your sails, it's already Saturday. Your man will have to work quickly to discover his information before the day's end."

"Bloody hell! I didn't stop to consider that!" Summerfield's eyes narrowed. "But he'll get what he needs before Sunday. I'll bribe him if I must. And by thunder, if Drummond's trying to pull a fast one, I'll do my damnedest to ruin his standing in business circles."

The absurdity of such a threat obliged Justin to swallow a bubble of laughter. In his opinion, any attempt on the earl's part to malign Drummond's reputation as a canny businessman was liable to fall on deaf ears.

Sorely tempted to tell his cousin that with a host of dunsters hounding him he was in no position to cast stones, the Major bit his tongue.

Eight

The coach bowled along Oxford Street, bound for Hanover Square. Annabel stirred uneasily. The closer they drew to St. George's Chapel in George Street, the lower her spirits dipped. Little wonder. In just over an hour she was expected to marry a man she detested.

She gave a deep sigh. Thanks to that scaly turncoat, Kenneth Boswell, her brilliant plan to hide away in Tunbridge Wells had come to naught. Her cheeks warmed at the recollection of the humiliation she'd suffered when Papa dragged her from the public coach last Friday. And even though three days had now passed, she could not think of the incident without a faint shudder.

Nonetheless, a good night's sleep had restored her confidence. The following day she'd barged into her father's study, where he'd been closeted all morning with Colin McPherson, and told him she would not marry against her will. And if he didn't wish to make himself a laughingstock, he'd best call off the wedding.

Infuriated, Angus had shouted, "I hae yer best interests at heart. So dinna think to cross me. If necessary, I'll drag ye kicking and screaming inta the chapel."

Clearly, Papa had won that skirmish, Annabel conceded dryly. Curious as to why the carriage now moved at a snail's pace, she peered out the coach window. They were nearing Oxford Market. The wide street was jam-packed with carriages. On the sidewalks, hawkers shouting their wares intermingled with morning shoppers eager to make their selections before the fresh produce was picked over.

"Och, lass, dinna be dooncast. 'Tis no a funeral ye be attending. 'Tis a bonny wedding."

Annabel cast him an exasperated look. "Really, Papa! You may regard it as a bonny occasion, but I do not. Indeed, I would not be here in my finery, had you not threatened to deliver me to the chapel in my shift, did I refuse to don the wedding gown you commissioned."

"Och, naught weel blame me? Satin and lace be very dear."

Annabel's eyes narrowed. Papa would have her believe that ingrained parsimony had driven him to bully her into compliance. But she didn't think so. Something other than her upcoming wedding was cutting up his peace. What exactly troubled him, she couldn't say. However, the memory of the long faces worn by both her father and Colin McPherson when she'd invaded Papa's inner sanctum on Saturday continued to nag.

She cast him a sidelong glance. In keeping with the solemn occasion he wore a black superfine suit of dittos, a style favored by wealthy merchants who apparently felt a matched coat and trousers added to their consequence.

Smiling faintly at the conceit of the male of the species, she marveled that she had not lost her sense of humor, given recent events. She absent-mindedly ran an index finger across the cool satin of her wedding dress, trimmed with yards of Belgium lace. The sensual feel of satin engendered a delicate shiver. Indeed, despite her ill-natured carping, the ecru satin gown *was* undeniably lovely. Nor would she soon forget the dressmaker's enthusiasm at the conclusion of the final fitting.

"*Ma foi, mademoiselle.* Ze gown has turned out well, *n'est ce pas?*"

"To be sure, Madam Reynard, you've outdone yourself," she'd hastened to say, resolutely swallowing the cynical thought that a funeral shroud would be more in keeping with the sham marriage about to take place.

As the carriage turned into Harwood Place, a surge of panic washed over her. It seemed incredible that she was about to marry a man she neither liked nor trusted. Four months ago, she'd brimmed with confidence that she'd be able to change Papa's mind. No such luck. She'd tried every ploy she could think of. Nothing had worked. Far worse, her father's woolly-headed conviction that he'd arranged a splendid match had gradually worn down her resistance.

Indeed, the reason she'd meekly donned her wedding dress this morning was that she'd grown weary of fighting a losing battle. The inevitability of her marriage weighed heavily upon her as the coach drew to a halt before St. George's Chapel.

Still, as she descended the coach steps, she raised her chin a notch. True, her fate was sealed. Like it or no, she'd soon be the Countess of Summerfield. However, that did not mean she planned to surrender her hard-won independence. Indeed, as a married matron, she'd be free to go her own way—something society frowned on in the case of unmarried females.

A nasty little smile tugged at the corners of her mouth. With luck, no whisper of her investments in the stock market would ever reach the earl's ears. Thus, if their marriage became intolerable, she needn't meekly endure it.

Her smile vanished at the thought of Kenneth Boswell. The traitor! He'd violated her trust and she fully intended to sever the connection. The sooner the better!

* * *

Major Camden left the rooms he'd let in Conduit Street at ten o'clock on the dot. The sun was shining, but not too hotly. The air was scented with apple blossoms. All in all a perfect day for a wedding, he conceded glumly. George Street was only a short walk away. Swinging his cane jauntily, he set off on foot.

However, by the time he approached the chapel's central portal, he was leaning heavily on the cane and his lips were set in a grim line.

"Pardon, Major."

Turning, Justin recognized the earl's valet. "Is something amiss?"

Danvers shook his head. "Naught that I'm aware of. His lordship wishes your company in the vestry. If you will follow me, I'll take you to him."

"By all means lead the way."

Led into the sacristy, Justin hastened to take refuge in a Queen Anne chair and stretch out his leg before he glanced at the earl, who flashed him a grin and asked, "How do I look?"

The major cast a discriminatory eye over his cousin's attire and manfully resisted an urge to shudder. While the earl's gray doeskin breeches were unexceptional, the cut of his Jean de Bry coat was designed to make his narrow shoulders appear broader. An experiment Justin adjudged a miserable failure. Especially as the coat was done up in a bilious shade of plum which called unwelcome attention to his cousin's florid complexion.

Suffice to say, a flamboyant streak that bordered on the eccentric had long plagued the Camden family. More than once Justin had thanked his stars he was a career officer confined to wearing a uniform for the most part. The restriction saved him from all manner

f worldly fads that had the unfortunate tendency to
make one look ridiculous.

"Well?" asked the earl, still preening.

Justin cudgeled his brainbox, seeking something in-
nocuous to say that wouldn't be an outright fib.

"New coat, I collect. Weston?"

The earl shook his head. "Weston cut up nasty about
what I owe him. So I switched to Nugee. He designed
my waistcoat as well."

Justin gave an involuntary shudder. He'd done his
best to ignore that very item, chiefly because he considered it an even worse sartorial travesty than the ill-cut
plum coat. Indeed, the crimson satin waistcoat, embroi-
dered with a floral pattern in silver, rendered him momentarily speechless. Furthermore, once he regained
his voice, he deemed it prudent to change the subject.

"Seeing you all decked out in your finery, I take it
you've decided to go through with the wedding."

Summerfield snorted. "I'm not such a fool as to whis-
tle away a fortune."

Justin arched an eyebrow. "You've heard nothing
from your solicitor?"

"Not a word." Summerfield sighed. "With my luck,
he won't show up with his report until I'm standing
before the altar with the cream of the *ton* peering over
my shoulder."

"That's cutting it pretty fine, is it not?"

The earl nodded just as Danvers barged in to announce it was time for his master to move to the altar
and for the major to take his seat in the front pew.

Bidding his cousin adieu, the major went outside and
walked round to the front entrance, grateful his leg no
longer throbbed. When he stepped through the outer
columns he encountered a crush of latecomers waiting
to be ushered to their seats.

Not the least of those latecomers was Sally, Lady Jersey. The heiress, whose nickname was Silence because she never stopped talking unless obliged to draw a breath, hailed him. Justin groaned inwardly. One of the reasons he shied away from tonnish affairs during his long convalescence was this very matron.

The dark-haired beauty had attempted to get her claws in him while he was still on crutches and in no mood for dalliance. At a time in his life when he'd wondered if he'd end up a helpless cripple, his feelings had simply been too fragile. He'd shrank from testing his virility in a passionate affair with the fickle countess, who ran through lovers at a pace that would make any sensible man's head spin.

"La, Justin, your timing is perfect. I shall adore making an entrance on the arm of such a handsome officer."

Justin snorted. "Gammon! How are you this fine morning, my lady?"

"Splendid! But do call me Sally. It is your prerogative to decline becoming my lover, but surely we can cry friends?"

As one of the patronesses at Almack's, Lady Jersey would make a formidable enemy. But what the hell! He was due to leave for Portsmouth at week's end, so if she managed to lure him into his toils before then, more power to her.

Justin gave a bark of laughter. "I'd be mad to turn down such a generous offer. Friends it is then, Sally."

"Excellent. Now then, what do you make of this misalliance? I am persuaded your cousin has a flare for the dramatic. Do you not agree?"

The major blinked. Had perchance Lady Jersey somehow got word of Summerfield's atrocious waistcoat? But no. Dramatic was not the precise word to describe the crimson monstrosity. Melodramatic would be infinitely more apt.

Puzzled at to what precisely she was driving at, he ventured with wry caution, "In common with beauty, I fear drama is in the eye of the beholder."

"Very well, rogue, play the innocent. Everyone knows Summerfield's been punting on the River Tick for years. And now this eleventh hour rescue from debtor's prison. Of course, he's obliged to pluck his heiress from the merchant class, but needs must when the devil drives, *n'est ce pas?*"

The countess might chatter like a magpie, Justin mused sardonically, but every once in awhile she threw in a poser just to keep the listener on his toes.

"Obviously, you sympathize with the social-climbing baggage."

Justin opened his mouth, but his blanket denial was forestalled by Lady Jersey, who tapped him smartly on the chest with the sticks of her closed fan and chided, "Really, major, one might suspect you had a tendre for the gel."

The possibility that Sally Jersey might just be a true clairvoyant sent an icy chill skittering up his spine. "Don't be ridiculous. I scarcely know her. I merely think it unfair to judge her so harshly. While it's true her father owns a merchant fleet, on her mother's side Miss Drummond's lineage is unexceptional."

"La, I do believe I've hit a nerve. It's rumored that Miss Drummond is a connection of the late Lady Winthrop."

"For once a rumor is true. She's her granddaughter."

Sally Jersey's eyes glittered with triumph. "It is like pulling teeth to get any information out of you Camdens. The entire lot of you is as close-mouthed as oysters."

Justin could kick himself. In his zeal to champion Annabel, he'd forgotten to guard his tongue.

"You should have spoken up sooner," the countess

scolded. "A granddaughter of a marchioness casts an entirely different light on the subject."

Had his slip of tongue worked to Annabel's advantage? he wondered. He prayed such was the case.

"Still, the gossipmongers can't wait to tear her apart. What a pity you'll be in Portugal, Major, and unable to shield her from their venom."

"Regrettably, I must set off for Portsmouth Friday next. However, you'll be here to lend her countenance—should you so desire."

Lady Jersey regarded him with raised eyebrows. "La, Major, you've more crust than a pieman. Dare you suggest that I take her under my wing?"

Justin cast her a lazy grin. "As one friend to another, I'd be most grateful if you did. But you must suit yourself, of course."

Nine

Justin stepped through the main portal. St. George's Chapel buzzed with low-keyed chatter emanating from both sides of the aisle. He glanced at the attractive woman on his arm who for once was living up to her nickname. He was most anxious to see her seated so he might slip into the front pew before the bride entered.

After scouring each and every row on the groom's side, twin worry lines quirked just above the bridge of his aquiline nose. All he found were spaces he couldn't pry the svelte Lady Jersey into with a shoe horn. Disconcerted, he toyed with the idea of asking her if she'd mind sharing a pew with a merchant on the bride's side. However, one glance at the countess's haughty demeanor convinced him she'd snap his head off if he dared.

Frustration mounting, he was almost at wit's end when a cough fraught with meaning penetrated his consciousness. A glance in that direction netted Lord Jersey. With alacrity, Justin led Sally over to her notoriously tolerant husband, who'd had the good sense to save his wife a seat.

Once rid of the albatross round his neck, the major felt almost lighthearted as he walked on. He reached the front pew and slid into the seat next to the aisle—just in time to watch the bridegroom saunter nonchalantly past the chancel rail and assume his familiar languid pose before the altar.

Justin frowned. Damn his eyes! Must he be so blasé? The earl's insouciance bordered on sacrilege. A marriage based solely on greed and lust—at least on the part of the groom—could never hope to bring happiness to the bride.

The twin lines above the bridge of Justin's nose formed deeper ruts. He could not speak for the bride, of course. For all he knew, the idea of being a countess had turned Annabel's head. Still, he hoped she wasn't being coerced by her father in to wedding his scapegrace cousin.

He shook his head to clear it. Justin wished it were within his power to call the whole thing off. But he had no say over the matter. Having met Angus Drummond, he adjudged him to be bound and determined that the wedding take place. Nor would Summerfield dream of halting the ceremony—not without a compelling reason. There was simply too much at stake.

The music coming from the church organ segued into the wedding march. That and the collective "ah" murmured by the assembled guests signaled the entrance of the bride on her father's arm. Justin's first impulse was to twist his head round, but he could not bear to be caught gawking like an ill-mannered dolt. Thus, he was forced to rely on stiffnecked pride to keep his eyes facing front, even though he was dying for a glimpse of her. It seemed like an eon passed before he sensed her presence as simultaneously the scent of apple blossoms filled his nostrils. Casting a sidelong glance, his heart turned over. She looked exquisite in satin and lace. The gown's vanilla cream shade heightened the rich peach-color of her cheeks. Its fitted bodice outlined pert, young breasts that stirred the major's loins as she glided past.

For a second or two, he feared the bride's father would plow right into the somber-faced vicar. Instead, he halted in the nick of time. Justin was much struck by the contrast between Annabel's aristocratic profile and her father's homely features. Beauty and the beast, he mused.

What wrung his heartstrings was the wistfulness in Annabel's eyes as she looked at her father's withdrawal. His emotions in turmoil, Justin's fingers curled round the edge of the wooden seat in an effort to firmly anchor himself in place—even as he fought down an almost overwhelming urge to snatch up the bride and race from the chapel with her safe in his arms.

A random cough from the congregation jolted him back to grim reality. Forced to come face to face with the ironic situation he'd innocently become embroiled in, Justin honestly didn't know whether to laugh or to cry. Choosing the former, his shoulders shook with suppressed laughter, tinged with bitterness at the losing hand fate had dealt him. He could just imagine the fiasco that would ensue should he attempt to abduct her. Given his bum leg, he'd be lucky if he didn't drop her. Hell, he'd be lucky if he didn't trip over his own cane.

His macabre sense of humor gave way to gloomy resignation. Best leave well enough alone. He might see Annabel as an innocent lamb dragged before the sacrificial altar against her will, but common sense whispered not a single guest would agree with him. Besides, it was too late to halt the proceedings without creating a scandal. All he'd succeed in doing was making himself a laughing-stock.

"Dearly, beloved . . ."

Justin did his best to ignore the vicar's voice. Devil a bit! He wished he'd realized beforehand how painful it would be to witness the ceremony. It was far more nerve-racking than standing one's ground during a battle charge. Tempted to bolt, his honor demanded he not turn tail.

The squeal of the vestry door as it swung inward drew Justin's gaze as the earl's man of business came into view. The spineless minion paused at the threshold until he spotted his quarry, then sidled up to the altar.

The obviously-affronted vicar posed the question on everyone's tongue. "Sir, what is the meaning of this interruption?"

"I beg your indulgence, sir," squeaked the timid solicitor. "And yours, too, my lord. However, I think you should peruse my report before proceeding further."

He thrust a single sheet of paper toward Summerfield, who accepted it with one eyebrow cocked. "Better late than never I suppose," he observed dryly.

Watching his cousin's face darken with anger once he'd scanned the report, Justin was seized with a terrible sense of foreboding. The earl crumpled the single sheet of paper and trained his wrath upon the father of the bride.

"Why you mealy-mouthed blackguard! Those four ships you claimed to be expecting sank off the Cape of Good Hope a month ago. You knew on Friday that you are a bankrupt, did you not?"

Angus Drummond's bulging eyes looked ready to pop. He stretched out both hands, palms upward, in a placating gesture. "Nay, ye dinna ken. I'll uphold my side o' the bargain. I just need a wee bit more time."

"Poppycock! You tried to ram this marriage down my throat knowing you're penniless." Summerfield shoved Annabel toward her father with enough force to make Drummond stagger. "Take back your daughter. I wouldn't marry her now if you doubled her dowry," he snarled.

As the Scotsman struggled to keep his footing, Anna-

el disentangled herself and took a step apart from her
ather.

The audience tittered. Anxious for her well being,
ustin scanned Annabel's face. He fully expected to see
umiliation reflected in her dark blue eyes. Instead he
aught a flicker of profound relief.

Justin was still pondering her odd reaction when a
nervous giggle from one of the guests was followed by
scattered laughter. The exact moment it dawned on the
earl that he'd suddenly become a figure of fun, his
normally florid complexion drained of every drop of
ts color.

His pallor alarming, he fixed his gaze upon Justin
and said grimly, "Good day to you, cousin. I'm off before I murder this cursed pinch-penny for making a
fool of me in the eyes of my peers."

The earl cast a final glare at the Scotsman before he
strode toward the side door.

Angus raced after him, imploring, "Dinna be daft,
mon. If ye dinna marry her, I'll sue for breach of promise."

Despite the major's ferocious scowl, issued with the
intent of restoring order, spontaneous peals of laughter
escaped from the round-eyed crowd. But as far as Justin
was concerned the final straw was the feckless wag who
cackled, "Came to see Summerfield leg-shackled. But
dammee, if it ain't a three ring circus."

Justin cast a wary glance in Annabel's direction, just
in time to discern her dawning horror over the fact that
her father's questionable business dealings had just
been aired in public. Far worse, the groom had jilted
her at the altar with the cream of the *ton* bearing witness.

Annabel blanched and might well have toppled had
not Justin been there to catch her. Lifting her into his
arms, and thankful his leg was up to the strain, he

carried her through the side door into the deserted ves
try where he carefully deposited her in a padded arm
chair. Not wishing to intrude further, he'd already
started to move away when she caught hold of his hand
Instantly, he went completely still.

"Thank you, Major," she whispered.

Justin glanced down at her, his heart in his eyes as
he slowly lifted her dainty hand to his lips and brushed
it with a feathery kiss before regretfully releasing it.

She gazed at him as if trying to see into his soul. "It
was good of you to rescue me from all those prying
eyes. I don't think I could have endured hearing their
mocking laughter another second."

His back ramrod straight, Justin walked over to the
vestry window and peered out. He watched his cousin's
coach pull away from the curb. Justin turned to face
the rejected bride, thinking how odd it was that the earl
had spurned the one woman in the world that his heir
would give his eyeteeth to call his own.

"No thanks necessary," he drawled. "It's not often I
get to rescue a damsel in distress."

Annabel responded with a shaky smile. "How odd
that we only meet when one of us is about to take a
spill."

Justin cast her a wry grin. "The memory of my infamous one will go with me to my grave."

"So I would imagine." Her dancing eyes sobered.
"You look fit. Your leg has properly healed, has it?"

"Well enough that I'm off to rejoin my regiment on
Friday."

"I collect you like army life."

"It suits me. Rest here while I seek out your father."

"I shouldn't advise it. Papa's liable to snap off your
nose. He finds it hard to see reason when he's in high
dudgeon."

Justin awarded her a wry grin. "If so, he's met his match in my cousin."

"You and the earl are related?" She gave an odd little laugh. "Silly question. You sat in the front pew, did you not?"

"As heir presumptive, it was expected of me. Though had you wed my cousin, I believe I'd soon be out of the running."

Annabel's dark blue eyes twinkled. "Rest easy, Major. Judging by today's events, your destiny as heir presumptive seems secure."

Grinning, Justin shrugged. "Believe me, inheriting an earldom is not something I pine for. Now then, would you like me to find you a cab?"

"No need. Papa's coach is nearby."

The room's atmosphere seemed charged with something indefinable yet precious. Still, given the circumstances, Justin knew it would be folly to linger. He bowed and turned his back on the lovely Annabel Drummond.

He'd almost made good his escape when she called after him softly, "If our paths don't chance to cross again before Friday, God speed, Major."

Justin hesitated in mid-step. The temptation to drop to his knees and declare his everlasting devotion was almost too strong to resist. Happily, some particle of sanity remained. Instead of making a cake of himself, his step only faltered ever so briefly before he passed through the outside door and closed it behind him.

Ten

The Court of King's Bench was situated in the south-east corner of Westminster Hall, opposite the Court of Chancery. Pale winter sunlight filtered into the courtroom from a handsome lancet window set high in the wall above the witness box, where the Earl of Summerfield stood squirming.

High on his dignity, a white-wigged, black-robed chief justice surveyed his austere domain from an elevated podium. Below him sat eight additional judges, all similarly attired, all equally pompous.

Viewing the proceedings from the visitor's gallery, Angus could scarcely contain his glee. True, it had cost him a pretty penny to procure the services of the counselor presently grilling his archenemy. But as he watched rivulets of sweat stream down the earl's gaunt face, he felt it money well spent.

Angus continued to muse. It had taken months to get his breach of promise suit on the court docket. Now they were within a stone's throw of final arguments. Yet he dinna have the slightest inkling as to how the case would turn out.

Angus scowled at nothing in particular. Some days he thought he'd lose the case; some days he thought he'd win; some days he considered it a toss up. Some days, he dinna ken what to think.

If he won, all would be rosy. Not only would he have

the satisfaction of getting back at the knave who'd jilted Annabel at the altar, the settlement awarded by the jury would amply compensate for the humiliation both he and his daughter had suffered.

His smug expression faded. Woe betide him if he lost. Not only would the culprit escape punishment, the loser must pay the winner's court costs. And for a man of his admittedly-parsimonious bent, having to shell out even more blunt than he had already, would rankle even more than an unfavorable verdict.

Excused from the witness box, Summerfield staggered over to the visitor's gallery where he collapsed onto a hard wooden bench as far from his avowed adversary as possible. Angus couldn't care less where he sat. The trial was approaching its climax. He dinna dare let his attention wander. Not with the defendant's counselor doing his best to knock holes in his breach of promise suit.

He listened with mounting trepidation as the earl's mouthpiece argued his client was within his rights to jilt his bride-to-be, because her father planned to welsh on his part of the bargain. Outraged by this exaggeration of the true facts, Angus studied the members of the jury, eager to gauge their reaction.

To a man, the freeholders' stony expressions gave no clue as to whether or not they'd swallowed the defense's argument. Frustrated, Angus glared at the barrister defending Summerfield. No question, the curst pettifogger was a slippery customer.

Indeed, Angus reflected that whoever had said, "The first thing we do, let's kill all the lawyers," had had the right idea. Because, loathe as he was to admit it, his own counsel was equally shifty.

Even so, his lawyer's virtues far outweighed his drawbacks. In particular, Angus was favorably impressed by the barrister's impassioned contention that jilting Annabel before the cream of society was unconscionable, and that the defendant deserved to pay through the nose for such an unwarranted insult to a gently-bred female.

Angus snapped to attention. Both sides having completed their summation, the case now passed to the jury. On pins and needles, he keep his eyes peeled on the jury box as they whispered amongst themselves. After ten minutes spent deliberating, the foreman rose to announce their verdict.

From his lofty perch, the chief justice inquired, "How does the jury find the defendant?"

"Guilty, my lord justice."

"Quite. Have you settled on a sum you consider just compensation for the scandal that has dimmed a young woman's prospects?"

"Aye, my lord, we have."

The chief justice asked peevishly, "Must I wring every word out of you?"

"Four thousand pounds is the sum we think fair."

Summerfield groaned and dropped his face in his hands.

"Four thousand it is!" cried the chief justice. Rubbing his hands together, he added with obvious relish, "Plus payment of plaintiff's court costs, of course."

While reimbursement of out of pocket expenses of the trial was customary, the chief justice's edict prompted the earl to issue yet another anguished groan.

Exactly the sum I advanced the cruel bastard upon signing the marriage contract, Angus silently crowed.

His euphoria faded. Had he lost the case, the shoe would've been on the other foot. Indeed, despite the welcome settlement, it would take a year or two of hard penny pinching before he fully recovered from the loss of his ships.

But at least he hadn't lost the case. In fact, he'd won it. Best of all, he thought with a vindictive smile, if

Summerfield couldn't raise enough rhino to pay every cent of the damages awarded by the court, he'd end up in debtor's prison. Which in Angus's admittedly biased opinion, was his just deserts.

A month after the trial, the tip of his nose reddened by exposure to the bitterly cold November day, Angus slid into a booth at Lloyd's and motioned for coffee. Seated opposite, Colin McPherson waited until his crony had ordered a second mug before trying to coax his fellow Scot out of a fit of the sullens.

"Depend upon it. By hook or by crook, Summerfield will raise enough blunt to pay you off."

"Damn right. Else he may rot in debtor's prison for all I care."

Angus idly scanned the crowded room. His affable expression underwent a sea change the instant he espied his archenemy standing just inside the entrance of the coffee room.

"Well, if that dinna beat the Dutch!" Angus exclaimed. "Summerfield's mouthpiece must ha'e sprung him from jail."

Impeccably attired in a midnight blue coat of Bath superfine, the Earl of Summerfield skimmed over clusters of the coffee drinkers in search of his Scottish nemesis. His usually florid complexion looked sallow, despite a fondness of spirits that never waned during his month-long sojourn inside Newgate Prison in the section known as Tangiers. Actually, he'd spent almost as much time imbibing ale in the prison's tap room as he had in his rented quarters.

However, although able to live in relative comfort whilst imprisoned, his release from jail was too recent to allow cheerless memories of a room without windows to fade entirely. Nor, he thought with a shudder, could he easily erase from his mind the indignity of being deloused yesterday afternoon by his valet.

He could well understand his servant's dismay at first sight of his master after a month in jail. The earl permitted himself a sardonic smile. On second thought, perhaps first smell was more to the point, he mused.

Never one to shirk his duty, Danvers had immediately set about scrubbing away all trace of Summerfield's incarceration. Also, thanks to the efforts of his excellent valet, the earl's Hessians were shined to a fare-thee-well and his crisply starched neckcloth was tied in an arrangement dubbed *Trone a Amour* by an euphoric Danvers.

Nonetheless, while the earl felt being well turned-out was a boost to his morale, he had more on his mind than his wardrobe. Before the day was much older, he meant to square accounts with Angus.

A reluctant smile enlivened his gaunt features. How ironic, that had his skinflint great uncle been more accommodating, the Earl of Summerfield need not have resorted to marrying a tradesman's daughter to replenish his coffers—an ill-fated notion that had resulted in his being thrust into prison. Yet he must not be bitter. Had not Greatuncle Bertie bequeathed the earl a hunting box in Leicestershire in the will, very likely he'd still be languishing in Newgate.

Instead, since hunting lodges were at a premium in the autumn months, his solicitor had been able to sell it for a handsome profit. The resulting windfall had enabled Summerfield to pay court costs, plus the hefty settlement awarded Drummond by the buffleheaded jury, with enough cash left over to bail himself out of jail.

His lips twisted in a rueful grimace. So here he stood,

bout to hand over four thousand pounds to a man
he'd much rather strangle. Summerfield grimaced. Unfortunately, strangulation was a hanging offense. Simply
put, either he paid up or he'd wind up back in prison.
Or worse, at the wrong end of a rope at Tyburn.

Squaring his shoulders, he marched over to Drummond's booth and presented him with a certified bank
note drawn on the Bank of England for the full amount
owed.

"Here's your blood money! I hope you choke on it."

Angus gave a rusty chuckle. "Och. Niver fear, I weel
put it to gude use."

"I don't give a damn what you do with it. However,
there's another matter between us that wants settling."

"I'm nae sure I ken."

"Then I must needs make my meaning crystal clear,
must I not?"

His pale blue eyes agleam with malicious glee, Sum-
merfield slapped Drummond across the face with a
York tan glove, and said in a voice abrim with menace,
"Your curst breach of promise suit impugns my honor.
I demand satisfaction."

Eyes smarting, Angus's hand soothed his stinging
cheek. "Are ye daft, mon? Duels are illegal."

"Blast the legalities. Either agree to meet me, else
I'll see you branded a coward."

Confronted by the earl's ultimatum, it dawned on Angus that in the normal course of things only the nobility,
and those of the gentry aping their betters, fought duels. Thus, to be asked to take part in a duel raised
Angus above the common herd. Ever ambitious to ele-
vate his social standing, he decided he'd be a fool to
turn down such a golden opportunity.

His barrel chest puffed with pride, Drummond said,
"Name your second. Colin will meet with him to iron
out the details."

The earl's eyes narrowed at Angus's enthusiastic response. Didn't the nodcock realize that he had about as much chance of emerging from the duel with his whole skin intact as an icicle in hell had of staying cold?

Summerfield ruthlessly squelched his uneasy conscience. His life had turned into a living nightmare, thanks to Angus Drummond. And the only way the earl could redeem himself in the eyes of his peers was to best his adversary on the field of honor.

Naming his own second presented a problem, Summerfield conceded. His former cronies were more likely to cut him dead than they were to stand beside him. It was too bad that Major Camden had rejoined Wellington in June.

He took a full minute to wallow in self pity before he designated a sycophant as his second—never mind that Summerfield secretly despised the toad eater who had stuck to him like a cursed barnacle during his recent travails.

Business concluded to his satisfaction, Summerfield left Lloyd's.

Eleven

Dawn flirted with the horizon as the coach turned off Upper Guilford and headed north on Gray's Inn Lane. Swiveling his head on his thick, truncated neck, Angus bestowed a look of gratitude upon his seat companion. Summerfield had wanted the duel to take place at Hounslow Heath, but McPherson had held out for the open fields adjacent to Bagnigge Wells.

Colin stared at Angus, clearly troubled. "Beyond a doot, this morning's work is the most bacon-brained start I can imagine. Why are ye doing this? Dinna ye ken that Summerfield's a crack shot?"

"Och, the divil fly away wi' ye! I'll nae show the white feather."

"Dinna be daft. Wi' yer right arm in a sling after target practice, nae body wad think less of ye if ye have the gude sense to withdraw."

Angus's jaw jutted at a belligerent angle. "I'll no do that. Niver!"

With an air of quiet desperation, McPherson raked his fingers through his thick mop of brown hair. "I dinna want your blood on my hands. Show some sense. Ye barely ken one end of a pistol from the other."

"Put a sock to it!" Angus advised through clenched teeth.

McPherson cast him a wounded look and lapsed into a sulky silence. Personally, Angus doubted he could hit the broad side of a barn at point blank range. But it dinna matter. Summerfield's challenge had raised his social standing several notches.

Angus frowned. Admittedly, up to now, all his schemes aimed at accomplishing this end had come to naught. Over time, he'd grown fond of his wife. Still, he hadn't carried her off to Gretna Green because he loved her, but because he'd regarded an advantageous marriage as a means to rise above his humble origins. Unfortunately, instead of gathering Angus to the family bosom, Lord Winthrop had disinherited Sophia.

Angus's lips twisted cynically. So much for the sanctity of the family unit. And so much for his naive expectations. He'd pictured himself basking in luxury. Reality had been bleaker. The first years of his marriage had been an endless struggle to make ends meet.

He gave a rusty chuckle. One would think his initial brush with the stone-hearted aristocracy would have taught him a valuable lesson. To the contrary, he'd let his overweening ambition play him false once again. He'd had his heart set on his daughter becoming a countess. Only this time, when Annabel had ended up jilted at the altar, Angus had turned the tables and forced Summerfield to pay through the nose for his ungentlemanly conduct.

The carriage rolled to a stop. In the murky light, a cluster of low-growing shrubs seem eerily lifelike as they swayed in the stiff breeze. Shivering, Angus gave a derisive snort and returned to his musings. Not only had Summerfield coughed up what he'd owed, the silly nodcock had challenged him to a duel—never dreaming he was affording Angus yet another chance to realize his life's ambition.

McPherson clutched his sleeve. "What a hellish spot. I wish I'd niver agreed to be yer second. Dinna ye ken the mon's oot to kill ye?"

Angus pried McPherson's fingers loose from his coat sleeve and smoothed the wrinkled fabric. He searched for a way to express his true sentiments without shocking his crony.

At last, he shrugged his shoulders and said, "If he kills me, 'tis nae great matter. I'll die a gentleman on the field of honor."

"Whisht!" exclaimed McPherson. "Ye cannot mean it. Think of Annabel."

"The lass has a shrewd head on her shoulders. She'll manage fine withoot me," he said with conviction. "Climb doon, mon. Yon eastern sky begins to pinken."

Alighting, McPherson cast a look around. "Humph! Place looks deserted."

Angus took off his sling and left it on the coach seat before he jumped to the ground. His feet planted a foot apart, he scanned the hay field.

"I came early on purpose. Gives me time for a wee breather to study the lay o' the land before Summerfield arrives."

Adrift in a romantic dream, featuring a knight on a white charger who bore a striking resemblance to Major Justin Camden, Annabel was reluctant to surface. But the voice calling her grew ever more insistent. Stubbornly, she managed to ignore it until the speaker gripped her upper arms and gave her a thorough shaking.

Annabel rubbed the grit from her eyes with her knuckles, then gasped as her intruder came into focus. "Aunt Sukie, what on earth are you doing here?"

"Pray excuse my rag manners. This is an ungodly hour to come calling. But 'tis a matter of life and death."

"Life and death? Whatever do you mean?"

Sukie opened her upraised palm to reveal a sorry-looking scrap of paper. "Read this. I found it crumpled into a ball on the hearth."

Annabel plucked the note from Sukie's palm and scanned it. Her eyes first widened then narrowed. "This has to be a hoax. Papa's too canny to fight a duel when he knows naught about firearms."

"My dear, I hate to disillusion you, but sometimes men act like bloody fools. I suspect this may be one of them."

"Nonsense!" Annabel scoffed. "Papa's arm is in a sling. He can't fight with a sprained wrist."

Sukie held up her hand. "Hear me out. Voices beneath my bedchamber window woke me. I reached for Colin, only to find him gone. I peered out the window barely in time to see him disappear inside your father's coach. But by far the most damning evidence is the note in your hand. It states time and place."

"All it says is that Papa will pick up Uncle Colin at half past five. It could mean afternoon, not morning," Annabel argued halfheartedly.

Sukie gazed at her with earnest concern. "Dearest, you are grasping at straws. Why else would Colin slip away so early without a word to me as to where he was going? And why else would your father agree to meet his archenemy at Bagnigge Wells of all places? Especially at such an unfashionable hour."

Aunt Sukie was right. Only a duel made sense, Annabel grudgingly acknowledged. "Did you bring your carriage?"

"Why yes, I did."

"Excellent. I must scramble into my clothes. Any hope of aborting this mad-brained scheme depends on how fast we can reach Bagnigge Wells."

* * *

No inner doubts rose to cut up Angus's peace as he waited for both their respective seconds to confer one last time before the duel took place. He'd already spoken to the surgeon who'd arrived a few minutes before. He'd even exchanged cool nods with Summerfield, who waited on the opposite end of the paced-off area.

Indeed, it was not until the mid-field conference between their respective seconds broke up and Colin rejoined him, that Angus experienced the slightest qualm in regard to the probable outcome of this morning's exercise.

Think of it! Death for him was likely mere minutes away. Actually, he didn't wish to think of it. Indeed it did not bear thinking of, Angus reflected. However, it was too late to change his mind, too late for regrets.

But even though he thought himself prepared to meet his maker, when McPherson actually handed him a silver-mounted flintlock pistol, a host of fresh misgivings rose up to plague him. Thus preoccupied, he inadvertently pointed the pistol toward Colin, who grabbed his arm and forced him to re-aim the gun barrel toward the ground.

"Careful where ye point that popper. 'Tis already half cocked."

"Och, mon," Angus protested as he rubbed his sorely abused limb. "Ye dinna ha'e ta be so rough. I'd no hurt a hair o' your head."

"I should hope not!" McPherson exclaimed, still a bit shaken. "Now then, the rules are as follows. You and Summerfield line up back-to-back in mid-field, each of you armed with a pistol pointed skyward. When you hear the command, you must take five paces before you may turn and fire. Is that clear?"

Angus's heart skipped erratically. Whatever possessed him to agree to this buffleheaded scheme? Not that it mattered. He must muddle through or be labeled a coward.

"Angus?"

"Aye, clear as crystal."

McPherson peered at him intently. "Ye dinna have to go through with this, ye ken?"

"Niver sae so. My honor depends on it."

While their seconds remained on the sidelines, both men approached mid-field. At the shouted command, each man cocked his pistol, took the proscribed five paces, then turned to face his opponent.

But as Angus wheeled round, he tripped, and as he fell, accidentally discharged his pistol. His bullet struck Summerfield's left shoulder. The astonished look on the earl's face had barely registered in Angus's brain as he regained his footing. He was not destined to remain upright for long. The earl's return fire traveled through Angus's chest to his heart, killing him instantly.

As the carriage came to a halt, Annabel peered out the isinglass window, just in time to see the Earl of Summerfield flinch as Angus's bullet struck him. She reacted with a nervous titter that would have appalled her under normal circumstances. Still, who would have thought Papa would actually hit his target? Especially with a sore wrist. Somehow or other, he'd managed the impossible feat. But Annabel scarcely had time to gloat before Summerfield took careful aim and pulled the trigger.

His bullet drilled a hole in Papa's chest. Blood spurted from the gaping wound. With an anguished moan, Annabel watched her father's stocky frame slowly crumble until he was lying on the field, his sightless eyes gazing skyward.

Horrified, Annabel leapt from the coach before the postilion had a chance to lower the steps. Kneeling, she cradled his head in her lap and pleaded, "Don't die, Papa. Please, please don't die!"

Annabel applied steady, firm pressure to the wound, trying to staunch the blood pouring from the hole in his chest. But it was no use. The blood kept right on gushing, kept right on soaking through the makeshift padding and trickling through the spaces between her fingers.

"Papa, Papa," she sobbed.

She was still rocking him ever so gently when the surgeon finished bandaging Summerfield's shoulder and trudged over to see how the other duelist fared.

"It is useless to rock him. He's dead, miss," he stated in a kindly tone.

Annabel knew he spoke the truth. Yet she wasn't quite ready to relinquish her father's body. She remained with his head tenderly cradled in her arms until McPherson intervened. Refusing to stand for any nonsense, he pulled Annabel to her feet and led her over to his carriage, where he gave her a hand up.

"Take her home, Sukie. I'll follow in the Drummond coach as soon as I claim the body."

Huddled inside the coach as it rumbled over the cobblestones, Anna stripped off her bloody gloves and tried not to dwell overmuch on her bloodstained gown. The temperature of her skin vacillated wildly, at times so cold it raised goosebumps, at times so feverishly hot and clammy that she longed for a bucket of ice water to be dumped over her head.

Annabel was oblivious to almost everything—save her overwhelming grief. Even the revolving coachwheels seemed to be saying: *Papa is dead. Papa is dead. Papa is dead.*

Bone-weary, Annabel leaned back against the squabs and closed her eyes. Even when she covered her ears with her hands, it was no use. She still heard the same refrain.

Summerfield resisted an unseemly urge to give a rousing cheer as the Drummond coach bore away Angus's body. Even the knowledge that he was now obliged to flee England to avoid prosecution failed to dampen his spirits as he climbed into his own coach and signaled his coachman to drive on.

"I trust your wound is not serious, my lord?" remarked the toad eater who'd acted as his second.

"Not at all. A mere scratch," Summerfield assured him.

But in that assessment, the earl proved to be in error. Two days later, infection set in and he developed a raging fever. Still, he hung on for a fortnight before gangrene carried him off to his maker.

Twelve

Annabel had been poring over a ledger for over an hour when the figures began to run together. With a sigh, she pushed back her straight chair and stood. While she needed to grasp the intricacies of Papa's shipping business as quickly as possible, there was no point in going blind. At least, that's what she told herself as she paused to wrap her Kashmir shawl more tightly around her chilled shoulders.

She strolled over to the French doors and peered out at the walled garden. Stripped bare of greenery by harsh winter storms, the scene was further blighted by piles of soot-tinged snow. Its bleakness matched her mood.

With Papa's death, she'd inherited two merchant vessels. Despite Uncle Colin's belief that she was capable of taking over the reins and rebuilding the fleet, she was plagued with doubt. Perhaps, she thought, instead of learning the business, she ought to sell it.

Suddenly appalled at her defeatist line of reasoning, she turned away from the window. It wasn't like her to turn her back on a once in a lifetime opportunity to prove her mettle. Nor did she want to—not really. She was still depressed over her father's death, that was all. Doubtless, she'd soon come about.

She shot a fulminating glare at the stingy fire in the fireplace. With Papa gone, she might please herself. Crossing to the bellpull, she gave it a good yank.

"You rang, miss?"

She nodded at Fenton. "I'm tired of freezing in my own home. Send a footman to build up the fire in here and, from now on, tell the staff to keep healthy blazes going in the rooms I frequent."

A half hour later found Annabel sipping tea in front of a cheerful blaze, her frame of mind much improved.

Fenton entered. "Major Justin Camden desires a word with you, if at all convenient."

His cousin had died two weeks after Papa, Annabel recollected. Doubtless, he'd come home to assume the title.

"I see. Show him in, Fenton. Then bring a fresh pot of tea."

Annabel detected the major's manly tread scant seconds before he crossed the threshold. The anxiety in her midnight blue eyes vanished once she saw him none the worse for wear—despite the recent siege of Burgos.

Smiling at him, she observed, "Such nasty weather. Come warm yourself before the fire, Major."

Justin felt as if he'd suddenly come home. Emotion formed an unwieldy lump at the base of his throat. He managed a painful swallow. It'd been eight hellish months since he'd last laid eyes on her, he reflected as he gazed at her hungrily.

God, how he desired this woman! He wanted to make passionate love to her for hours on end. His loins ached for the wanting of her.

Many a night he'd lain awake thinking of her after battling the French all day. Of late, he'd begun to wonder if he'd exaggerated her beauty. On the contrary, she was even more beautiful than he remembered, especially with her glorious titian hair backlit by firelight.

Two long strides placed him before her. Standing so
ose, he couldn't help but notice an underlying sadness
her gaze.

"I understand your father passed away last Novem-
er. Allow me to express belated condolences."

Annabel gazed up at him intently, then sighed. "Given
at your own cousin died as a result of the same asinine
uel, I suppose I should reciprocate. But any such ex-
ression on my part for a man who killed my father and
ted me strikes me as the height of hypocrisy."

Justin gave a dry chuckle. Lord, how he'd missed her
rt tongue! "Totally unnecessary, I assure you. Godfrey
sued the challenge—not your father."

London was full of beautiful women, Justin conceded
he bent over her hand. But precious few of them
ad Annabel's fierce honesty or her intrepid spirit.

As he took her hand, a tremor passed through Anna-
el which she hoped to heaven he didn't notice. Not
ntil Justin released her hand and went to stand with
is back to the hearth did she regain a semblance of
ontrol over her seesawing emotions.

Beaming her a smile, he said, "As you see, I'm quick
take advantage of your offer. Believe me, ma'am, on
ich a day, a fire is most welcome."

A footman entered with a freshly-brewed pot of tea
nd a platter of macaroons, then stole away quietly.
nnabel scarcely noticed. Her dark blue eyes were too
tent on admiring the major's manly figure.

Having warmed his backside to his satisfaction, Justin
rned to face the fire. He stretched out his hands to
arm them in the heat rising from the crackling fire.
taring into the flames, his thoughts grew pensive.
Vhat with France's enforced retreat from Russia,
ere'd been talk of establishing a second front in either
olland or Hanover. Declining to head it, Wellington
ad entrusted Major Camden with a secret document

outlining his audacious plan for driving the French out of Spain entirely.

Two days ago, Justin had delivered this document to the British Government, then slept the clock round before visiting his solicitor and, second but hardly least, the lovely Miss Drummond.

"Tell me, Major, am I correct in assuming you've put your soldiering days behind you?"

"Upon my honor, you are mistaken!" Whirling round to face her, he was quick to soften his denial with a rueful grin. "After fighting the frogs tooth and nail for four straight years, I plan to stick by Wellington until we achieve victory."

"Then you're only home on leave? You're lucky you could be spared."

Justin suspected the main reason Wellington had granted him leave was that he'd needed a trusted courier to act as a go-between between himself and the British government. But, of course, his lips were sealed on that head.

"With both sides in winter camps, my presence isn't vital until the snow melts and the roads dry out. So Nosey kindly granted me a short leave to take care of pressing estate business."

Annabel's brow wrinkled. "Can you actually handle your responsibilities as the new earl in the time allotted?"

Justin thought of the tangled financial mess his late cousin had left behind and was obliged to quell a shudder. If only he could manage to scrap together sufficient funds to bring the run-down cottages on the country estate up to snuff, he'd feel better. But as things stood at present, he must lease out the Summerfield town house for the London season, then use the resulting nest egg to make the most urgent repairs before next winter.

"I'll do what I can, then leave the rest in the hands of my solicitor."

Annabel frowned. Did he mean Boswell? Not that it was any business of hers, of course. But still . . . she gave herself a firm mental shake and calmly changed the subject.

"Major, I'm about to pour myself a cup of Bohea. Care to join me? Or would you like something stronger?"

His pale blue eyes twinkled. "A cup of tea would be delightful."

"Excellent. Do be seated. I think you'll find the gold-striped silk wing chair comfortable."

With swift, catlike grace, the major assumed the chair indicated. Annabel managed to pour him a cup of Bohea without spilling a drop. She shot him an inquiring glance. "Sugar?"

"Yes. Two lumps please."

She added the requested amount, then handed him the china cup cradled in its saucer. As he took it from her, his fingertips brushed the edge of her hand, sending a delicious tremor coursing through her. Shaken, she swiftly lowered her gaze in the hope of hiding her sensitivity to his slightest touch. What was it about this particular man that so unsettled her?

In her frantic search for a fresh topic, curiosity triumphed over good sense. "Tell me, Major, is Boswell still your solicitor? Or have you engaged a new man of business?"

"I wouldn't dream of it! I have the highest regard for Kenneth's business acumen." Justin gave a rueful chuckle. "In fact, I daresay he'll do a better job of sorting out my affairs than I would—were I free to assume my duties as earl immediately."

"You trust him?"

"Implicitly."

"Really! I hope you will not live to regret it as I did!"

His demeanor thoughtful, Justin set his empty cup and saucer on the tea tray. "Kenneth claims you dismissed him due to a misunderstanding."

"Misunderstanding?" Annabel sputtered indignantly. "No such thing! The wretch betrayed me!"

"Betrayed you? Miss Drummond, if you mean to imply that Kenneth is dishonest, I find that hard to swallow."

"His honesty was never in dispute. Nor, to be fair, was his business savvy. Still, I was obliged to turn him off. He proved to be . . . untrustworthy."

There was a short leaden silence in which Justin determined he simply couldn't afford to drop the subject. After all, he was about to return to the Peninsula and leave his business affairs solely in Boswell's hands. Which, should it turn out that Annabel had a valid reason for dismissing him, wouldn't do at all.

"Kenneth considers your action unjust. He claims he was caught between the devil and the deep blue sea. He says he felt honor-bound to see that no harm came to either your person or your reputation."

"What he did was disloyal. Naturally, I sacked him. Since I could no longer trust him, I had no other choice."

Justin eyed her skeptically. "Miss Drummond, I don't like to press you, but it is important to my peace of mind. How percisely did he betray you?"

Thoroughly disgruntled, Annabel snapped, "Oh very well. I'll tell you the whole. Rather than let Papa coerce me into marrying Summerfield, I decided to lay low in Tunbridge Wells for a time. Unfortunately, I made the mistake of informing my man of business of my plans, who, instead of holding my direction in confidence, took it upon himself to tell my father. Which made it possible for Papa to find me before I had a chance to cover my tracks."

"Ah, the light dawns!" Justin exclaimed. "Your plan

to hide in Sussex was thwarted by Boswell's quick ⸱
So you retaliated by cutting the connection. Righ⸱

Annabel nodded.

"Wasn't your response a trifle harsh?"

Hurt by the disapproval she read in his gaze, she thrust her chin forward. "I despise talebearers. In my opinion, he received his just deserts."

"Come, come, Miss Drummond. Kenneth did what he did to protect you from possible harm. Given the circumstances, do you not feel your dismissal was unwarranted?"

Annabel eyed him coldly. "Sir, to keep an employee I no longer trusted would be the height of folly. Now, I hope we may retire a subject which begins to bore me."

Noting her frosty demeanor, Justin decided there was no sense in pursuing the matter further. After all, she *did* have the right to sack anyone in her employ, if she so chose.

Determined to lighten the mood, he cast her a dazzling smile featuring even white teeth that stood in stark contrast to his weather-tanned face.

"I beg your pardon for being tiresome. I assure I didn't call on you with the intention of pulling caps."

Annabel arched an eyebrow. "Did you not? Why then did you come?"

"Why to see how you are faring. Only recollect the last time our paths crossed, my ramshackle cousin had just seen fit to jilt you at the altar. I wished also to express my condolences for the loss of your father."

She cast him a searching look. "Are those your sole reasons for calling, Major?"

Justin flushed and dropped his gaze. He felt like a schoolboy caught filching sweets behind a harried cook's back. He'd come because he couldn't stay away a minute longer. He desired her with every fiber of his being. Before he'd inherited the earldom, his scruples over his lack of prospects had held his desires in check. But now, his circumstances had changed. Still, it was too early in the game to confess he'd come courting. Or was it?

All of a sudden, he couldn't bear the thought of leaving for Lisbon without knowing if Annabel returned his sentiments. Justin drew a ragged breath and rose to his feet.

"I came because you haunt my dreams. I came because I ache for you. I came because I wish to court you."

Annabel's jaw dropped. "Are you mad? I'm in mourning."

"Rest easy, my dear. I do not intend to begin courting you this instant. It would hardly be fair, since I must board a Lisbon-bound ship in a few days."

"T-then why speak of this at all, Major?"

Annabel gazed up at him saucer-eyed as he rapidly closed the distance between them. He cast her a rakish grin.

"Because, my dear Miss Drummond, you take my fancy. And before we are a minute older, I mean to find out if the feeling is mutual."

Before she could utter a word of protest, Justin pulled her to her feet and boldly embraced her. The instant his lips claimed hers Annabel became caught up in a powerful current of pleasurable sensations. When he finally lifted his mouth from hers, she whimpered in protest.

Justin slowly released her, then took a step backward. He stood with his feet planted a foot apart, peering down at her, his hands clasped behind his back.

Annabel regarded him as if she were seeing him through a hazy mist, the epitome of all her girlish fantasies. "Y-you kissed me."

"So I did. Tell the truth. Did you like it?" he asked huskily.

"Y-yes, but . . . it's most improper."

He gave a shout of laughter and kissed the tip of her

Allow us to proposition you in a most provocative way.

GET 4 REGENCY ROMANCE NOVELS *FREE*

An $18.49 Value

PRESENTING AN IRRESISTIBLE OFFERING ON YOUR KIND OF ROMANCE.

Receive 4 Zebra Regency Romance Novels (An $18.49 value)
Free

Journey back to the romantic Regent Era with the world's finest romance authors. Zebra Regency Romance novels place you amongst the English *ton* of a distant past with witty dialogue, and stories of courtship so real, you feel that you're living them!

Experience it all through 4 FREE Zebra Regency Romance novels...yours just for the asking. When you join *the only book club dedicated to Regency Romance readers,* additional Regency Romances can be yours to preview FREE each month, with no obligation to buy anything, ever.

Regency Subscribers Get First-Class Savings.

After your initial package of 4 FREE books, you'll begin to receive monthly shipments of new Zebra Regency titles. These all new novels will be delivered direct to your home as soon as they are published...sometimes even before the bookstores get them! Each monthly shipment of 4 books will be yours to examine for 10 days. Then, if you decide to keep the books, you'll pay the preferred subscriber's price of just $3.65 per title. That's $14.60 for all 4 books...a savings of almost $4 off the publisher's price! What's more, $14.60 is your <u>total</u> price...there's no extra charge for shipping and handling.

No Minimum Purchase, a Generous Return Privilege, and FREE Home Delivery! Plus a FREE Monthly Newsletter Filled With Author Interviews, Contests, and More!

We guarantee your satisfaction and you may return any shipment...for any reason...within 10 days and pay nothing that month. And if you want us to stop sending books, just say the word, you're under no obligation.

Say Yes to 4 Free Books!

COMPLETE AND RETURN THE ORDER CARD TO RECEIVE THIS $18.49 VALUE. ABSOLUTELY FREE.

(If the certificate is missing below, write to: Zebra Home Subscription Service, Inc., 120 Brighton Road, P.O. Box 5214, Clifton, New Jersey 07015-5214

4 FREE BOOKS

Yes! Please send me 4 Zebra Regency Romances without cost or obligation. I understand that each month thereafter I will be able to preview 4 new Regency Romances FREE for 10 days. Then, if I should decide to keep them, I will pay the money-saving preferred subscriber's price of just $14.60 for all 4...that's a savings of almost $4 off the publisher's price with no additional charge for shipping and handling. I may return any shipment within 10 days and owe nothing, and I may cancel this subscription at any time. My 4 FREE books will be mine to keep in any case.

Name _____

Address _____ Apt. _____

City _____ State _____ Zip _____

Telephone ( ) _____

Signature _____
(If under 18, parent or guardian must sign.)

RF1095

Terms and prices subject to change. Orders subject to acceptance by Zebra Home Subscription Service, Inc.

An $18.49
value.
FREE!
No obligation
to buy
anything, ever.

elegant nose. "You have me there, sweetheart. However, I meant no disrespect. You see, I needed a kiss to keep me warm on bitterly-cold nights which seem to be a soldier's lot."

He gazed at her tenderly. "Will you write to me, Annabel?"

Her expressive dark blue eyes mirrored her thoughts. Part of her longed to oblige him; part of her shrank from the impropriety.

Justin cast her a soft smile. His dearest love was in over her head. Though tempted to tease her, he scrupulously refrained. "Very well, my darling prude, I won't press you. But mind, should you ever need to get in touch with me for any reason, Kenneth Boswell has my direction."

Annabel bristled and the sand castles she'd been building in her dreams were ruthlessly swept away by a chilling tide of suspicion. How naive could she get? He and Boswell were close as inkle weavers, for God's sake! No matter how much it pained her, she must pluck out her tender regard for Major Camden before it was too late!

Too late to undo the damage, Justin bit his tongue. Why had he mentioned Boswell at such a crucial juncture? Heartsick, he reached out to his beloved, wanting to soothe her ruffled feathers. But, instead of falling into his arms, Annabel shrank away from him, almost as if she considered him to be contaminated by his close association with Boswell, Justin acknowledged sadly.

Annabel's suspicions proliferated. Boswell felt he had a score to settle with her. Why not advise Major Camden to woo and wed her in order to get his hands on her fortune?

"You must think me very stupid not to realize at once that Boswell is behind this bogus courtship, Major. I think you'd better go."

Justin dug in his heels. He wasn't about to stand idly

by and watch something he considered infinitely precious disintegrate before his eyes without a pitched battle.

"Not until we clear up this misunderstanding that threatens to cast a blight on a promising relationship."

Anxious to be rid of him before she disgraced herself by bursting into tears, Annabel said grimly, "Major, if you don't leave under your own power, I shall see you forcibly ejected."

"I do not particularly relish drawing your frail butler's cork. But I don't intent to budge an inch until you explain what's put your back up."

Annabel glared at him. Would he knock Fenton down if she dared summon him? Not wishing to have her butler's untimely demise on her conscience, she reluctantly bowed to the inevitable.

"Very well, sir. Since you insist, when you mentioned Boswell, I suddenly realized 'tis all a sham. You don't wish to court me because you admire my character. What you want is to get your hands on my money."

Gravely offended, Justin stiffened. "What? Devil a bit! How dare you cast aspersions on my honor?"

For a second or two, Annabel wavered. What if she were wrong? What if his professions of admiration were heartfelt? But, of course, that was only wishful thinking on her part. Depend on it! The cad was after her fortune. And Boswell had put him up to it!

"Do not think you will turn me up sweet with your play acting. I'm on to you now, sir. It is all a pretense."

His skin flushed with anger, Justin doubled his fists. "The hell you say! If there's any disillusionment to be suffered, I'm the blind pigeon. To think that I was in awe of what I thought was your sterling character makes me nauseous."

For a tense millisecond, Annabel feared he was so angry he might actually strike her. Thus, his elegant bow surprised her. Straightening, he cast her such a look of withering scorn that it put her in a quake.

"Good day, vixen. Rest assured, I shall not trouble you further."

With that, the breath-takingly virile Major Camden marched with perfect military precision from the room. Left behind, Annabel flinched when the front door slammed, then slumped into the same chair she'd urged on him when the atmosphere between them had been warmer.

She stared at the dying embers of the fire, knowing she should call a servant to build it up. She was too exhausted from the emotional seesaw she'd been riding to move so much as a muscle.

As for the suspicions that had inflamed her, surely she was right to call the major to book for his deceit. Was she not? A single tear trickled down her cheek as she concentrated on forcing her chin to quit wobbling. Common sense told her not to believe the major's protestations of innocence. Yet she couldn't help but wish that her suspicions were without merit. Certainly, she conceded, the major had appeared thunderstruck when she'd accused him of being a fortune hunter.

What if she were actually mistaken in her scathing assessment of his character? What if she'd sent an honorable man into battle believing that she thought him unworthy of her regard?

Merciful heavens! She must stop tormenting herself. Right or wrong, it was too late to mend matters. For all intents and purposes, Major Justin Camden had washed his hands of her.

Her chin jutted belligerently. Not that his rejection mattered a fig. Annabel was used to fending for herself. And if she was destined to live out her life as a spinster, so be it!

Thirteen

Brussels June 1815

After Waterloo, the question most often put to Major Justin Camden by armchair generals was: "Why attend a ball with the enemy on your doorstep?"

The question never failed to rankle. Chiefly because having served as one of Wellington's aide-de-camps since his return to active duty in 1812, he'd come to hold the Iron Duke in the highest esteem.

However, on the evening of the Duchess of Richmond's ball, though he'd never dream of admitting it to a living soul, Wellington's coolness in the face of the alarming dispatches he was being peppered with had so dismayed Justin that he'd put the very same question to his fellow staff officer, Lord Fitzroy Somerset, who'd explained that the ball was the place where every British officer of rank could be found, making it easy to quietly issue orders during the course of the evening without unduly alarming the civilians.

"Besides, before quitting headquarters," Somerset added, "Nosey alerted all his troops to be ready to march at a minute's notice."

Thus, reassured that his idol knew what he was doing, Justin entered the Richmonds' rented house in the rue de la Blanchisserie in a more or less optimistic frame of mind. The room boasted hangings in royal colors of crimson, gold and black and pillars wreathed in ribbons, leaves and flowers. But the major was not interested in the decor. Nor was he interested in dancing with any of the lovely young ladies. His sole interest was Wellington himself. With furrowed brow, he examined the crowded dance floor and then, not finding his quarry, began a detailed study of the various nooks and crannies hugging the shadowy corners. There he discovered several enterprising officers bidding fond adieu to wives and sweethearts.

In the end, Nosey's idiosyncratic braying laugh gave his location away. Justin spotted him chatting with Lady Georgiana Lennox.

"Yes, the rumors are true. We are off tomorrow," said Wellington, nodding to Justin as he joined them.

The rest of the evening passed in a haze. Officers whose regiments were any distance away quietly slipped off as the night advanced. Shortly before supper, a dispatch was brought in by Lieutenant Henry Webster from Quatre Bras for the Prince of Orange. Slender Billy handed it unopened to Wellington. The message announced the repulse of Prussian forces from Fleurus on the road north-east of Charleroi. Having digested this enlightening but grim news, Wellington recommended the prince return at once to his field headquarters.

At supper, Justin marveled at Wellington's ability to keep up an animated conversation despite the grim dispatch that had sent the Prince of Orange back to Quatre Bras on the double. However, once the meal ended, Wellington asked Justin to inquire of his host if there was a decent map on the premises.

Eager to oblige, the Duke of Richmond led Wellington into his study and spread out a map. Wellington looked at it, then said wryly, "Napoleon has humbugged

me, by God! He has gained twenty-four hours' marc
on me."

Newly alarmed, Justin asked, "What shall you d
sir?"

"I have ordered the army to concentrate at Quati
Bras; but we shall not stop him there." He jabbed h
thumb-nail at a point on the map just south of Wate
loo. "I must fight him here."

Justin felt immeasurably better. One reason Wellin
ton won so many battles was that he always ferreted ou
the best possible site before engaging the enemy. On
of Justin's duties as aide-de-camp was to reconnoite
the surrounding countryside, and he recognized th
spot the Iron Duke had pinpointed. A week ago, he'
led Nosey to the very spot so he could take a loo
around.

London, June 1815

Almost there, unless she'd misread the landmark:
Annabel didn't think she had though. Not when ever
thing looked so poignantly familiar.

"Achoo!"

She cast a sympathetic glance at the young woma
seated beside her. Poor Fanny. Flowers invariably mad
her eyes water and itch, and Annabel had brought alon
a bunch of violets to lay on her father's grave. A wav
of sadness enveloped her. But for that stupid duel Pap
might have lived to a ripe old age. The duel had bee
fought though, and despite her best efforts, she'd bee
helpless to prevent it. She took a deep, fortifying breat
to stave off the searing spurt of anger she invariabl
felt whenever she recalled how he'd died.

Annabel resolutely stiffened her lower lip. To dwe
on the senseless duel was pointless. Orphaned thre

years ago, she'd managed well enough on her own. She cast a fond smile at Fanny. Her first order of business had been a ladies' companion to lend her countenance. She'd ended up hiring her favorite teacher, Miss Francis Bolton, who'd taught mathematics at the seminary Annabel had attended in Bath until she'd turned seventeen.

From the onset, the arrangement had worked out better than she had a right to expect. Annabel had soon realized what a treasure she'd acquired. Dearest Fanny had a head for numbers equal to hers. Indeed, Miss Bolton had proved to be an excellent sounding board for Annabel. Why, even Uncle Colin never ceased to be amazed at how she'd managed to dramatically increase the profits of the company her father had left her, whilst at the same time contracting for two more ships to be built by a master craftsman at Plymouth.

But the secret of her astounding success was no mystery to Annabel. Soon after she'd engaged Fanny's services as a sop to convention, she'd come to appreciate her companion's true worth. Thanks to Fanny, who was temperamentally more cautious, Annabel, impulsive by nature, had come to see the value of looking before she leapt. Indeed, she shuddered to think how she would have fared in the business world without her companion's excellent counsel.

With a rueful smile, Annabel recalled the battle royal that had raged before she'd finally convinced Fanny she was entitled to a modest share of the company's profits. The argument which finally turned the tide was that at thirty, Fanny must hedge her bets. Five years a spinster on the shelf, her marriage prospects were abysmal. With no widow's jointure to count on, she must needs salt away funds against her retirement.

Annabel's smile took on a rueful note. To be sure, she'd provided generously for Fanny in her will, but times were uncertain. Should Annabel marry, it was entirely possible her husband would refuse to honor her wishes. Not that she thought she ever would marry.

Three years ago, eligible bachelors had come beating on her front door. Aware most, if not all, were fortune hunters, she'd rejected the lot. Annabel grimaced. She'd so resented being under her father's thumb, she'd vowed to never again be any man's pawn. Regrettably her decision not to marry ruled out motherhood.

Even so, she doubted she'd ever change her mind. Of course, none of her suitors were Major Justin Camden, whom as far as she knew was still in the army. Probably in Brussels, she theorized. Oddly enough, despite the accusations that had torn them apart, should he ever come courting again, she candidly admitted she'd have difficulty rejecting his suit, but reject it she must. Although her suspicion that he was a fortune hunter had diminished with time, she had no ambition to follow the drum. Annabel felt that a marriage without mutual interests and genuine affection on both sides would ultimately fail.

Besides, Annabel reveled in being financially independent. Thus, at seven-and-twenty, she'd come to regard herself as a confirmed spinster.

"Achoo!"

A guilty flush stole across Annabel's face when she saw that the tip of her companion's nose had reddened. "My dear Fanny, I should have insisted you remain in London instead of dragging you off to Richmond."

"Fustian! My job is to accompany you wherever you go."

"Goose! Never at the expense of your health. Next time I shall take one of the maids."

Fanny's lively brown eyes twinkled. "You mean to play the tyrant?"

"Indeed, I'm prepared to be as highhanded as Bonaparte himself, if that's what it takes to make you see reason.

Fanny shuddered. "Pray don't mention that odious bully in my presence."

"As you wish," Annabel agreed.

The closed carriage halted next to the church. Handed down by a footman, Annabel insisted Fanny remain close by the carriage while she went on alone.

Her gaze fell upon the bunch of violets in her hand. The delicate blooms were a long-time favorite. A bitter-sweet smile flickered upon her mobile features as she recalled that before Napoleon's abdication he'd said, "I return with the violets of spring."

In March, he'd made good his promise, Annabel conceded with a small shiver. Boney's escape had stirred up the French once again and forced England to hastily reassemble the army they'd just demobilized. Her friend, Nathan Rothschild, had raised the necessary funds. In April, Wellington had established headquarters at Brussels, where he was now amassing an allied force to meet Napoleon.

Papa, Annabel recalled, had been inordinately fond of violets as well. Kneeling, she bowed her head and prayed for his soul. Even more fervently, she prayed that God grant her the tolerance to forgive him for dying so needlessly.

Heart heavy, she laid the violets on her father's grave. Their scent lingered as she turned and walked back to the carriage where Fanny stood waiting.

London, Autumn 1815

The heady aroma of fresh-ground coffee beans brewed to perfection met Justin as he followed Kenneth Boswell into Lloyd's Coffee Room.

The solicitor had the decency to wait until a pot of fresh-brewed coffee was delivered and poured before he began to pepper Major Camden with questions.

"So, what have you been up to the past three years?"

Justin thought the question specious but decided to answer it anyway. "Serving Wellington. Most recently at Waterloo."

Boswell appeared dissatisfied with his answer. "Yes, yes, I collect you fought at Waterloo. What I'm dying to know is why you didn't return to English soil at war's end in eighteen fourteen."

"I was asked to stay on as aide-de-camp to Wellington when he posted to Paris. There, I discovered I disliked politics and decided to sell out. Castlereagh begged me to escort the duke to Vienna first. We'd barely arrived when we heard of Napoleon's escape. Naturally, I postponed my homecoming to escort the Iron Duke to Brussels, where I rejoined his staff."

"But now you're home for good, right?"

"Of a certainty!"

Boswell grinned. "Stands to reason. You are, after all, the present Earl of Summerfield."

"Yes," he admitted ruefully. "So I am."

"You don't seem overjoyed," Boswell observed. "Surely you are not still pining for army life?"

The major repressed a shudder as he recalled the afternoon of June 15th when Ney's Chasseurs had trapped him and Wellington behind enemy lines. Galloping for their lives, they'd been forced to jump over a ditch packed with Picton's Highlanders.

"Ninety-second, lie down!" Nosey had shouted as he and Justin sailed over scores of hastily-retracted bayonets.

On worst mounts, Justin reflected with another shudder, they would never have escaped injury. Just the memory of their close brush with death still gave him nightmares.

"Not at all," Justin informed Boswell firmly. "With Boney tucked away for good, I'm perfectly content to retire from the lists."

"Really? Then why so blue-deviled?"

Justin snorted. "The sorry state of the property I've inherited would discourage anyone. To be sure, I knew my predecessor bled the property dry. Even so, I was genuinely shocked by the deterioration I found when I finally mustered the courage to visit the family seat. Most of the tenants have long since left. Those that remain live in squalor."

"What of the land itself?" asked Boswell.

"Criminally mismanaged for at least a decade," Justin announced gloomily. "It will take a genius to put it back in good heart. Especially with inadequate funds to finance farming innovations."

Boswell had the grace to look chagrined. "I'm sorry the funds you received from rental of the London house didn't stretch further. But I obeyed your instructions to the letter. Rest assured each cottage received a coat of whitewash and a rethatched roof."

"Devil a bit! I was not criticizing your handling of my affairs. You did well, given my meager funds. It is just that I'm in something of a quandary as to how to proceed now that I'm here to take over the reins."

"Well, if the task before you proves too onerous, as the last of your line you can break the entail, should you so desire."

Justin took a fortifying sip of strong, rich coffee. "I know I can, but it is the last thing I want to do. Surely there's some other recourse."

Boswell's eyes grew calculating. "I do believe I know where you can lay your hands on four thousand pounds, provided your scruples aren't too nice."

"The devil you say! Just what are you driving at?"

Boswell licked his lips as if savoring a treat. "Allow me to refresh your memory in regard to the circumstances surrounding your cousin's death. When Drummond sued for breach of promise, the jury awarded him four thousand pounds, and court costs. Pockets to let, your cousin ended up in debtor's prison. However, Summerfield did not remain at Newgate. A relative fortuitously died, leaving him the means to square his debts. Once released from prison, after paying Drummond off, Summerfield challenged him to a duel. Drummond died on the spot. Summerfield lingered a fortnight before he succumbed to putrid infection that prevented his wound from healing."

Justin regarded the solicitor with a raised eyebrow. "Kenneth, is there a point to this dreary tale?"

"Of course there is. With both duelists dead, guess who ended up four thousand pounds richer?"

"Miss Drummond?"

"Just so. She also inherited her father's merchant fleet. And by thunder, I have to hand it to her," Boswell admitted, grudgingly, "she's increased her inheritance three fold."

"Pity she'd already dismissed you from her employ," Justin commiserated. "I daresay if you were still her solicitor you'd be crowing instead of grumbling."

"Yes, well, I've grounds to grumble. Taught her the ropes, so to speak. But that's gratitude for you."

Justin suspected Boswell was exaggerating his role as mentor but held his peace. "Are you suggesting I woo Miss Drummond in order to recover the money the court awarded her father?"

"Most definitely! Where else can you lay your hands on the blunt you need?"

A wave of disillusionment washed over Justin as he recollected his quarrel with Annabel, who'd accused him of courting her for mercenary reasons at Boswell's suggestion. At the time, Justin had staunchly defended his friend, because he'd believed him a man of integrity. But now, too late to mend the breach, he realized that he'd stuck his neck out for a man of questionable ethics. And lost his beloved as a result.

"Forget it!" he snapped. "I've more pride than to stoop to such tactics."

"Forget pride. Forget scruples. Your back's to the wall. You cannot afford either," Boswell advised.

His ability to judge another's character badly shaken, Justin spoke with studied percision. "My honor's irreplaceable. I refuse to tamper with it."

Boswell gave a derisive snort. "Suit yourself. Just don't come crying to me when you have to place the entire estate on the auction block."

Fourteen

A few days after his enlightening conversation with Kenneth Boswell found Justin at Brooks', an exclusive gentlemen's club located in St. James's street. A club whose membership fee he'd not be able to swing, given his slim funds. But fortuitously for him, his predecessor had paid membership dues through 1817, and the club's committee had courteously informed him he was welcome to avail himself of club privileges at no additional charge for the next two years. So here he sat in one of the club's commodious leather chairs with his nose buried in the *London Times,* obstensibly reading but actually deep in thought.

Frankly, the realization that he'd lost Annabel's regard by siding with Boswell curled his liver. Two long years had passed since he'd set eyes on her. Yet, despite his anger over her insulting opinion of his scruples, not a day passed that he didn't think of her. Neither did a day pass that he didn't wonder how she was faring. Nor did a day pass that he didn't torture himself with the thought that she'd married someone else.

Quite suddenly, the newspaper he held was swept aside.

"What the deuce?" Justin demanded of his unseen tormentor.

"Home from the wars are you, Major? Though by rights I should now refer to you as my lord."

Justin's ferocious frown fled the instant he recognized his mischievous hassler. He gave a crow of delight and jumped to his feet.

"Scrope Davies! Ever the joker, I'll be bound."

"Fustian!" Davies scoffed. "No fair hiding behind the august *London Times*. It is meant to be read, not act as a shield."

Scrope Berdmore Davies Esq. was not just a handsome wit, he was a professional gambler. An intimate of both Byron and Hobhouse, he used his superior intellect to calculate odds and thus excelled at hazard, from which he derived a partial income. Even more astounding, he was a fellow of King's College, from which he received lodgings and an annual stipend for teaching during the Michaelmas term at Cambridge.

"One does not expect to see you in town during the little season, Scrope. Have you resigned your post?"

Davies chuckled. "No such thing. A mere flying visit I assure you. In the mood for company? Or should I restore your newspaper to its former position?"

Justin rolled his eyes. "To think I actually missed being the brunt of your acerbic humor."

"Spanish coin, Major?"

"Not at all." He reassumed his seat and waved Davies into an opposing chair. "I daresay we could have used you at Waterloo to buck up our spirits."

Scrope cast him a wry look. "If my current losing streak doesn't end soon, I may well end up fleeing to the continent. But enough of my paltry concerns. What are you doing in town? Thought you'd retired to your estate in Rye."

"So I did. But I found Camden Manor in such a shambles, I hied back to town to raise the ready to fix it."

Davies cast him a speculative look. "Do you hope to

be lucky in cards? Can I tempt you into a game of hazard."

The major gave a mirthless chuckle. "Find yourself another pigeon to pluck, old stick. I mean to sell the town house in Little Brook Street."

Davies whistled. "Which will no doubt fetch a bundle. Clever lad that you are!"

Justin shunted the dubious compliment aside. At three-and-thirty, he'd left his boyhood behind him long since. Nor did he feel the least bit clever.

"Actually, I'm loath to sell the house. But where else will I find the money to finance the innovations needed to bring my country estate to a pinch above snuff?"

Davies laughed. "You could always dangle for an heiress."

"Ha! No heiress wants a man with a slight limp and pockets to let."

"Balderdash! You're a better prospect than I am, and I've been attempting to woo one."

"What, give up your fellowship to get leg shackled? Surely you jest?"

Davies shrugged. "I doubt I shall have to resign my post at Cambridge. The young lady in question scorns my suit."

"Does she by God? A handsome fellow such as you? Tsk. Tsk."

"Care to try your luck with the reluctant heiress? I'd be happy to introduce you before I retire from the lists."

"No thanks. I'm not in the market for a wall-eyed wench, be she as rich as Midas."

Scrope snorted. "Do you actually think an antidote would tempt me to forsake my prestigious fellowship? I assure you the gel's a fair treat to look at."

"All the more reason why I wouldn't dream of poaching on your preserves."

"You won't be. Courting her is too dashed fatiguing.

Miss Drummond may be pretty as can stare, but she just ain't sociable. It is hard to woo someone who shuns society."

Annabel Drummond? Justin's heart beat a little faster, though he took care to hide it. "Your heiress is a recluse?"

"Not precisely. Just deuced elusive. I finally managed to cross paths with her at Sunday services."

"Pray, don't keep me on tenterhooks. What happened?"

"Froze me with a glare so icy the mere recollection of it brings on the shivers," Davies averred, his demeanor mournful. "Nothing for it but to slink back to Cambridge to lick my wounds."

Silence fell. Justin allowed it to lengthen for a time but finally said, "I was at St. George's Chapel in Hanover Square when my cousin, the late earl, jilted Miss Drummond. Little wonder she's standoffish."

"Standoffish? The gel's a cursed ice maiden."

"Do you blame her? My cousin humiliated her publicly."

"That's as may be. But four thousand pounds is ample compensation for the slight. And besides, three years is too long to hold a grudge against men in general."

"Just so," said Justin.

Shortly before they parted, Scrope volunteered, "In case you decide to try your luck, the church she attends of a Sunday is Saint George's in Hart Street."

"I'll bear that in mind," Justin promised dryly.

"Can't miss it, old chap. Its spire is topped by a statue of George the First, commissioned—believe it or not—by Hucks the brewer."

Amused by his own anecdote, Scrope Davies was still chuckling as he took his leave.

Left to his own devices, Justin took pains to review

his options. He'd been mulling over matters since his
recent chat with Kenneth Boswell. Running into Scrope
Davies clarified matters.

A wry smile flitted across his face. Justice must be
served. His honor demanded that he make up for the
slight Annabel had received from his predecessor by
making her his countess.

But he mustn't fool himself. Winning her hand would
be an uphill battle, especially since they'd parted ene-
mies. At the time, her lack of faith in his character had
stung. However, after yesterday's encounter with Kenneth, Justin was now forced to concede that her decision
to sack Boswell had been sound.

Even so, spinsterhood for the delectable Annabel
would be a tragic waste. It was his sacred duty to work
his way back into her good graces. And this time round,
he had no intention of taking no for an answer.

His motives were not entirely altruistic. It certainly
couldn't hurt to have a clever wife capable of making
money hand over fist, could it? True, he hadn't con-
templated setting up his nursery quite so soon. Yet it
was his solemn duty to marry so that the Camden line
would continue. Besides, if his memory had not played
him false, Annabel was quite beautiful.

His train of thought took a dark turn. While true
that Annabel had tried to wiggle out of marriage with
his cousin, in the end she'd agreed to marry a man old
enough to be her father. Why had she done so, if not
to gain a title? Might not the reason she was so cool to
Scrope Davies and her other suitors be that she was
hanging out for one? If so, no doubt she'd jump at a
second chance to become the Countess of Summerfield.

More often than not, Annabel attended Sunday services at St. George's in Hart Street, mostly because she

enjoyed walking in fine weather and it was the closest church to her house in Russell Square.

At present, she stood in a line that seemed to move at a snail's pace. Schooling her features not to betray her growing impatience, she discreetly shifted her weight from one foot to the other.

A step behind her, Miss Frances Bolton muttered in a disgruntled undertone, "Really, Annabel, this is outside of enough. Must we repeat this farce every Sunday?"

"I agree Mr. Hunt is notoriously long winded. Nonetheless, it would be quite rude not to compliment him on today's sermon before leaving."

"Nonsense! Heaping praise upon his head is the height of hypocrisy. The man's a mealy mouthed bore."

"Shh. We're almost within earshot," warned Annabel.

"Humph! Little I care if I'm overheard," Fanny grumbled. "For all we know a bit of candor might have a salutary effect on the pious jaw-me-dead."

Shocked, Annabel spun round to face her rebellious ladies' companion. "That will do, Fanny," she said with a hint of steel in her voice. "We are next. Pray keep a civil tongue in your head."

Miss Bolton sighed. "Oh very well. But I only do so to please you."

Annabel felt terrible. No matter how justified, whenever she rode roughshod over anyone, especially a friend, she ended up feeling mean-spirited. She was about to turn back toward Mr. Hunt, when she espied a tall black-haired man, who made her pulse quicken.

Heart pounding like a trip hammer, she blinked several times. The man standing before her bore a remarkable resemblance to Major Camden. Yet it couldn't be him. An Army officer wouldn't dream of appearing in public out of uniform. Thus, the fashionably dressed gentleman could not be the present Earl of Summerfield. Never mind that both the major and a man, who could well be his double, were extraordinarily attractive staring was unpardonably rude. Cheeks tinged pink with embarrassment, she forced herself to spin round to face Mr. Hunt, whom she found at last free to receive her.

"My dear, Miss Drummond, allow me to express my gratitude for your most recent donation. It will pay for the repair of the church bell as well as new altar cloths and heaven knows what else."

"Pray spare me my blushes. I'm just one of many contributors."

"You are far too modest. True there were others. But yours was far and away the most generous."

She felt the tips of her ears redden. Annabel scarcely knew where to look. How tactless of him to single her out for such lavish praise? To be sure, the sum she'd contributed had been generous but she could well afford it. Biting her tongue, she slowly counted to ten.

Composure restored, she uttered a few parting words before handing him over to Fanny, whom she hoped would refrain from knocking him down a peg, even though he richly deserved such a fate for making such a fuss over her donation when she'd have much preferred that he didn't.

Annabel took exactly ten steps before forced to halt. Confronted by the gentleman she'd stared at earlier, she was annoyed to find him lazily appraising her form. Blushing, she was even more annoyed when she felt the tips of her ears burning once again.

Justin regarded her with twinkling eyes. He'd forgotten what a willowy beauty she was. Just as he'd forgotten the strikingly vivid contrast there was between her flaming red hair and her dark blue eyes fringed with dark-red lashes. Admiring her, he decided that while the past week had proved frustrating, the young lady was well worth all the pains he'd taken.

After his discussion with Scrope Davies, he'd decided to court her. But first, determined not to be vanquished like all her other suitors, he'd discreetly followed her for an entire week. Said reconnoitering had revealed, that as Scrope had warned, Annabel didn't have a sociable bone in her body, which effectively ruled out running into her seemingly by chance at a rout or a ball or a musical evening in some private home.

Weekdays, she divided her mornings between her shipping office at the London Docks and the Royal Exchange. Aware that she was on bad terms with Kenneth Boswell, Justin did not think it wise to arrange a chance meeting at the Exchange. Nor could he come up with a valid excuse for frequenting the London Docks. With both sites deemed impractical, he could only be glad that, in common with most females, she liked to shop for clothing. She was also a prodigious reader, who visited Hatchards often to exchange her books. However, although he'd haunted the famed literary coffee shop the past week, Annabel hadn't shown up there.

Which had put him in a quandary. Neither his time nor his resources were infinite. London was expensive and an aristocratic pauper must watch every penny. He could not afford to linger in town, not with all the work waiting to be done at the Camden estate in Sussex. So, much as he regretted not having sufficient time or resources to woo her properly, he'd finally decided that he must somehow contrive a whirlwind courtship. And although he misliked waylaying her at her house of worship, because somehow it seemed to him to be faintly sacrilegious, he'd reluctantly concluded he must do just that.

"Well met, Miss Drummond." Justin lifted his top hat. "As beautiful as ever, I'll be bound.

Annabel hesitated. "Major Camden?"

Justin bowed. "At your service, ma'am."

Her generously-full lips curved in a bemused smile even as she darted a furtive glance at his leg. "How are you, Major?"

"Tolerably well." He awarded her an ironic grin. "Permit me to assure you that I've long since tossed away my cane."

"Excellent news."

He did look fit, Annabel decided, which came as welcome news. Despite their acrimonious parting, the possibility that he might suffer further injury in battle had been a constant worry.

Annabel swallowed the lump in her throat. "I believe I owe you an apology for casting aspersions on your character. I fear I've a deplorable temper."

Justin cast her a tender look of understanding. "I was equally at fault. Shall we cry pax?"

"I'd like that," she said, feeling suddenly shy.

Indeed, his masculine presence so overwhelmed her, she felt herself in danger of becoming addle-witted. And the troublesome creature was not even wearing the uniform that made many a feminine heart beat faster.

"You're not in uniform," she said, her voice faintly accusing.

"Just so, Miss Drummond. After Waterloo, I felt honor bound to sell out and assume the responsibilities that go hand in hand with the title."

Her heart did a crazy flip-flop. That ironic grin of his would be the death of her, she thought. Furthermore, the new earl was so handsome in his snuff-brown frock coat, gold brocade vest and tan trousers set off by his snowy-white neckcloth, that a single glance was enough to turn her knees to water. Annabel decided if she didn't make a clean break soon, she just might make a complete fool of herself by swooning.

"It was delightful running into you after all this time, but I fear I—"

"La, Annabel, I am persuaded the pious windbag could talk the hind leg off a donkey," Fanny complained as she reached her side. "How I long for a cup of oolong tea and the fresh-baked scones cook serves each Sunday."

Justin responded to this diatribe with a wry chuckle which commanded Fanny's attention. *Fudge!* thought Annabel. She'd hoped to avoid this encounter. Fanny was an incurable romantic, who could not understand why her employer was so adamant about avoiding the masculine sex—or at least those members of it that harbored amorous inclinations.

"Dear me. I did not realize I was interrupting a private tete-a-tete." Her cheeks stained a becoming rose, Fanny fixed her contrite gaze upon her long-time friend. "Pray forgive me, Annabel."

"Not at all. Fanny, allow me to introduce the former Major Camden, who is now the Earl of Summerfield. Major, that is, my lord, allow me to present my companion and friend, Miss Frances Bolton."

"Charmed," said Justin, bending over the pretty spinster's hand.

Annabel cast a worried glance at Fanny. The poor woman looked as if she were about to faint, which in a sense soothed Annabel's agitated spirits. The mere thought that she was the only female smitten with the handsome earl would have been quite insupportable.

Justin shifted his gaze to Annabel. "As Miss Bolton is longing for her tea, I shan't keep you. However, with your permission, I'll call on you one afternoon at your home in Russell Square."

It was on the tip of Annabel's tongue to refuse his request. Fortunately, her suddenly dry mouth prevented her from speaking without having a chance to think things through first. And once she had, she realized, in view of his past kindness to her at a time when she'd badly needed support, she could not summarily turn him away from her doorstep as she'd done all her other suitors.

Besides, it was an unpardonable conceit on her part to assume he still had courtship in mind after all this time, was it not? Indeed, she did not imagine he'd be such a fool as to allow her a second chance to reject him.

"But of course. Miss Bolton and I are generally at home on Wednesday afternoons."

"Wednesday, it is then, Miss Drummond." Turning to Fanny, he said, "Your servant, ma'am."

He awarded both ladies a boyish grin, then strolled off at what Annabel felt to be a remarkably jaunty strut for a man forced to hobble about on crutches a scant three years ago.

Turning to Fanny, Annabel smiled. "Come along, my dear. I, too, am in need for a bracing cup of tea."

Fifteen

Justin stood on the doorstep of the Drummond town house in Russell Square. During the intervening three days, he'd been too restless to sit still long. Nor did he sleep well nights. Constantly on the move, he kept remembering Annabel's slight hesitation before she'd issued her invitation. Almost as if she'd decided to grant him an interview against her better judgment.

He stared at the carved lion's head that adorned the door knocker. For certain, he didn't relish the idea of having his tendermost feelings trampled upon a second time. Yet he had to take that chance. Because, like it or not, his feelings were engaged, and he knew he'd never be at peace with himself unless he did everything in his power to win her heart.

He frowned. Much was at stake. He must take care to go slowly. Should he become too particular in his attentions before she was receptive, he sensed she'd retire into her shell. Standing a little taller, he ruthlessly shunted aside any further misgivings and lifted the door knocker.

A dour-looking butler opened the door.

"The Earl of Summerfield to see Miss Drummond and Miss Bolton."

The servant looked him up and down then grudgingly bade him enter. Mystified as to what had occasioned this unearned acrimony, Justin stepped into the

entry hall and cast a speculative look at the starchy but
ler.

"I am Fenton, my lord. Allow me to show you int
the drawing room where the young ladies await you.'

As Justin trailed behind the butler, he reminded him
self to proceed with caution. A veteran of many battles
he'd learned early to trust his instincts. The habit had
saved his neck many times over. And, at the presen
moment, his instincts were screaming that one step
wrong was all it would take to get him tossed out o
his ear.

It was something he could not afford to let happen
Now that he was home for good, the entire village ex
pected him to marry and raise a family. Justin didn'
mean to be finicky, but only the lovely Annabel would
do for his countess.

Ushered into the drawing room, he barely noticed
Miss Drummond's companion, despite the fact that Mis
Bolton's unadorned chocolate brown muslin served a
a perfect backdrop to gold flecks embedded in he
brown irises, which lifted her eyes above the ordinary
Nor did he note the ormolu clock that rested on th
Adam mantelpiece or the thick Axminster carpet, fea
turing a border of cabbage roses, or even the camelbacl
needleworked settee upon which the sole purpose of hi
visit—the titian-haired beauty—sat looking calm, cool
and collected.

Fortunately for Annabel, Justin was not a mind
reader, for Annabel was by no means as sanguine a
she pretended. Beneath the serene image she projected
to the world at large, her thoughts and feelings were in
a hopeless muddle.

Sipping her morning chocolate, she'd seen no reason
why Major Camden's impending visit should interfere
with her plans for the day. Consequently, after breakfas
she and Fanny had called at Hatchards, where she'c

been delighted to find Miss Austen's *Pride and Prejudice* waiting her perusal. The balance of the morning had passed in a whirlwind tour of milliner shops in search of new bonnets.

However, after luncheon, she'd begun to fret about what to wear when she received Summerfield, which wasn't like her at all. While she adored stylish clothes, her mind normally concentrated on weightier matters.

Nonetheless, to Annabel's stunned amazement, she changed her gown four times before she'd finally settled on her present ensemble, a long-sleeved gold silk creation made up in the French style, deliberately left open in front in order to reveal a white silk underdress with a hemline trimmed with three flounces.

Justin eyed her appreciatively. "My dear, Miss Drummond, you should wear gold more often. The color goes wonderfully with your red hair."

Annabel supposed she ought to be pleased he'd noticed her gown, since she'd had such trouble selecting it. Instead, for no rhyme nor reason, his compliment made her feel cross. She invited him to be seated and once he had, proceeded to pour tea from a burnished silver teapot. She handed the brimming teacup to her companion, who passed it along to Justin.

Accepting the steaming cup, he awarded Fanny a rueful smile. "I neglected to greet you, Miss Bolton. Forgive my deplorable manners."

Fanny cast him a startled look, then swiftly lowered her gaze. "Not at all, my lord."

Annabel's midnight blue eyes widened. She scarcely knew what to make of her companion's flushed cheeks, but couldn't seem to shake the niggling suspicion that Fanny found the earl every bit as attractive as she did. Yet she doubted the one-sided romance would prosper. Even if one assumed that the major was hanging out

for a wife, given the ramshackle estate he'd inherited
he'd be wise to marry an heiress.

Which was fine with Annabel, so long as he didn'
set his sights on her. Since Papa's death, she'd grown
used to her independence and marriage to anyone—
much less the forceful Major Camden—was all too likely
to cramp her style.

"Do try a macaroon, my lord," Fanny urged with a
shy smile. "Cook baked them especially today."

Annabel stared first at her companion, then at Justin
who shot Fanny a warm smile as he accepted the offered
sweet. *Was* it Fanny he intended to court this time
round? And what of Fanny? Had she set her cap for
the earl? Annabel experienced a most unsettling twinge
of jealousy.

Justin bit into the macaroon, pronounced it first oars
with him, then turned to Annabel. "Miss Drummond,
I've no wish to rake up unpleasant memories. However,
I was in Portugal when my cousin died. And although
granted a short leave, I had no time to flesh out the
details. I know, of course, that he and your father
fought a duel and that both died as a result. But I know
none of the particulars. Can I persuade you to shed a
bit of light on the subject?"

Annabel smothered a chagrined sigh. So much for
her suspicions. He hadn't come courting after all. "I'd
be glad to relate what little I know, but let me warn
you I'm only acquainted with the bare-bones of the
story."

"So many rumors floating about. I've no idea what's
true and what isn't. My understanding is that Summerfield lingered for some weeks after the duel, then died
as a result of a wound inflicted during it?"

"I assume so, but cannot say for certain. The last
time I set eyes on him was at the duel itself. Although

my father winged him, Summerfield remained on his feet."

Justin cast her an incredulous look. "You were there?"

Annabel flushed scarlet. He must think her a shameless hoyden. But it was too late now to recant. Her hands rushed to fan flaming cheeks.

"I realize my attendance was most irregular but I was frantic."

"I understand. Pray continue."

"Very well. One of Papa's business associates acted as his second. His wife came to me with a crumpled note detailing the particulars she found on the hearth. Since my father knew next to nothing about firearms, I rushed to Bagnigge Wells in hopes of halting the duel. Alas, I got there too late to dissuade Papa from such a freakish course. I saw him stumble, which explains how he managed to wing your cousin."

"Are you saying my cousin died of a minor wound that turned putrid?"

Annabel raised her chin a notch. "That is what I think but cannot say for certain, since I didn't nurse him. In contrast, the earl was a crack shot. He drilled a hole in Papa's chest, killing him instantly."

She recalled holding her father's head cradled in her lap. Close to tears, she said unsteadily, "If you don't mind, I . . . I would appreciate a change of subject."

"Much as I regret distressing you further, I feel I must ask if you know what precipitated the duel?"

Annabel sighed. "I suppose the money the earl was obliged to pay Papa stuck in his craw. I suspect he sought revenge."

"You think my predecessor challenged Angus Drummond to a duel he knew he'd win?"

Annabel shrugged. "It was common knowledge Papa didn't know one end of a pistol from the other."

"It is possible my cousin deliberately took advantage

of the situation," Justin conceded grimly. "What I can
not fathom is why your father agreed to meet him
Surely he realized that given his inexperience with fire
arms, the odds of survival were scarcely in his favor."

"To Papa, acceptance of the challenge raised hi
status to that of a gentleman. It never crossed his min
to refuse. Social ambition was his Achilles heel."

"I appreciate your telling me the facts as you know
them." Justin climbed to his feet. "I should like to invit
both of you ladies to take a stroll in the park with m
Friday afternoon, provided the weather remains balmy.

"Well, I . . ."

"Oh do say yes, Annabel," Fanny pleaded, her brown
eyes shining. "It has been a donkey's age since we'v
been accompanied by a gentlemen on our walks."

Justin studied Annabel's mobile features with amuse
interest. Clearly, the heiress was of two minds in regar
to his invitation.

"Yes, do say you'll come, Miss Drummond," he
coaxed. "As a special inducement, I promise to trea
you both to ices at Gunter's."

Dark-blue eyes warming, she said, "It is too bad o
you to offer such an irresistible bribe."

"Does that mean you'll come?"

Justin responded to her curt nod with an impuden
grin. "I must remind myself to cut the wheedle mor
often."

Moments later he was gone, leaving behind half
pot of cold tea and two young ladies who studiousl
avoided each other's eyes. A tiny frown disturbed Anna
bel's brow. While Fanny was three years her senior, a
times Annabel felt much older and definitely les
flighty. And yet Fanny was so level-headed in financia
matters, whereas Annabel was inclined to be impetuous
She supposed the sensible course would be to swap th
duenna role to suit the situation.

Annabel cleared her throat. "Fanny, I don't want you to take what I'm about to say amiss. However, I feel I should warn you that all Justin Camden inherited is a title. He'll have to have the devil's own luck to hang onto the estate he inherited from his scapegrace cousin—much less take on a dowerless wife."

Fanny bit her trembling lip. "Since you see fit to broach the subject, allow me to assure you I am not hanging out for a husband—much less a peer of the realm."

"My dear Fanny, I do humbly beg your pardon if I've misjudged your intentions. If all you are about is a lighthearted flirtation with the handsome earl, I trust I haven't spoiled things for you. It's just that I'd never forgive myself if I failed to point out the pitfalls, and you suffered hurt as a result."

Fanny attempted a smile but achieved something that more closely resembled a grimace. "I thank you for your concern, truly I do. But I see no harm in indulging ourselves on occasion with an agreeable male escort. Anyway, it is not his looks I find so taking. The major's hearty laugh reminds me a little of Peter."

"Oh, Fanny, do forgive me for being so mean-spirited."

"Goose! Truly I took no offense. Now then, I do believe a brisk walk round Russell Square is the very thing to shake off my megrims. Do you care to accompany me?"

When she declined the invitation, Fanny went for her walk without her. Left behind, Annabel felt terrible. She had no right to cut up Fanny's peace simply because she craved a bit of gaiety to brighten their somber existence.

Overcome with remorse, she let her mind drift. When she'd hired Frances Bolton as her companion, it had been with the understanding that the position would

be regarded as a temporary post because Fanny was
engaged to Captain Peter Shaw. At the time, the captain
was a member of His Majesty's navy fighting the upstart
Americans. They'd planned to marry upon his return
to England. But their plans had come to naught the
day an official dispatch arrived from naval headquarters
informing Fanny that Shaw had died bravely during a
naval engagement off the Maryland coast.

Annabel rose from her chair and went to peer out
the window at the daisy bush still giving off blooms
even though it was well into autumn. What had gotten
into her to badger Fanny, whose loyalty and affection
she treasured? As to Camden, she'd be willing to wager
he'd soon lose interest in two spinsters living on the
fringe of society, who could scarcely be said to lead scin-
tillating lives.

Sixteen

In the hall of the Drummond mansion, Justin announced, "I've only popped in for a minute, provided of course the ladies are ready."

"If his lordship will wait here, I'll inquire," Fenton intoned.

"Splendid."

Observing Fenton's ponderous retreat, Justin admitted it was not easy to remain affable in the face of the butler's prickly aloofness. Still, if at all possible, he was determined to win the servant's respect and approval. After all, one never knew when moral support from that quarter might come in handy.

He was more determined than ever to win the illusive heiress's hand. Justin permitted himself a faint grin. Wellington being his idol, Justin had decided to use some of the tactics the Iron Duke had employed on the battlefield.

First, he'd lull Annabel's suspicions. Then he'd lure her down the garden path with such finesse she'd never suspect he'd captured her heart until too late to reclaim it. After all, he reasoned, all's fair in love and war.

Justin groaned. God's life! What had possessed him to trot out all those trite chestnuts?

The rustle of silk alerted him to the imminent arrival of the ladies. His eyes lit up at the sight of Annabel wearing a lemon yellow muslin frock and carrying a

matching parasol. Her cottage bonnet of the same hue
set off her titian tresses to perfection.

"My dear Miss Drummond, what a vision you are in
pale yellow."

"Fustian!"

He frowned. For the life of him, he couldn't under
stand Annabel's aversion to flattery. Especially when it
was sincerely meant. Anxious not to start the outing off
on the wrong foot, he frantically searched for a way to
redeem himself. However, deliverance from an unex
pected quarter rendered his quest unnecessary.

"Dearest, Annabel," Fanny scolded, "you must learn
to accept compliments graciously."

"Hear! Hear!" Justin's eyes twinkled. "Miss Bolton
permit me to say you look all the crack in your lavender
silk."

Fanny thanked him prettily then addressed Annabel
"You see? What could be more agreeable?"

"What indeed?" Annabel responded dryly. A gleam
of mischief in her eyes, she addressed Justin. "Shall we
start afresh? You, my lord, look slap up to the echo in
your snuff brown riding coat and polished Hessians."

Justin's shoulders shook with suppressed laughter. So
the clever puss had turned the tables on him, had she
Well never mind. At least her companion had coaxed
her into a better humor.

"Touche, Miss Drummond." Grinning from ear to
ear, he offered an arm to Fanny.

Outside, the ladies spotted the open landau waiting
at the curb.

Justin assisted Annabel and Fanny into the carriage
before climbing in himself. Once settled opposite the
ladies, he signaled the coachman to proceed.

"Wherever did you run across such handsome equi
page?" asked Annabel.

"At Tattersalls. It was scheduled to go on the block

but I persuaded the head auctioneer to rent it to me for the balance of the little season."

"You intend to stay that long, do you?"

"Yes. I find the family coffers sadly depleted by the spendthrift who preceded me, so I must sell the town house in Little Brook Street in order to make urgently needed repairs at my estate before winter sets in."

"I see."

Annabel swiftly averted her gaze as she mulled over the kernel of information he'd tossed her. Had she misjudged his motives for renewing their acquaintance? Were her suspicions that he'd come courting in hopes of recovering the four thousands pounds the court had forced his predecessor to pay Papa totally unfounded? Or was his announced intention to sell his London property a feint designed to throw her off track?

Annabel honestly did not know what to think. Even more aggravating, she didn't understand why the likelihood that he'd *not* come courting depressed her spirits. One would think she'd be thrilled to learn he wasn't a fortune hunter, but was instead a man of integrity, who'd rather sell a prime piece of real estate than stoop to such tactics. Blue-deviled, she wished the emotional seesaw she seemed to be riding wasn't so nerve-racking.

Justin knew he should give himself a pat on the back. His sleight of hand had cast doubts in Annabel's mind as to his true motives. It wouldn't do to explain his intentions were entirely honorable just yet, because he sensed she still didn't trust him unequivocally, that she still had doubts as to his honesty. He found it troubling.

He rigorously shunted his qualms aside. He must not lose sight of his goals, the first being to sweep the lovely but skittish Annabel off her feet and marry her before she recovered her senses. The second was to rescue his inheritance from certain oblivion by selling his town house to the highest bidder.

At Hyde Park, the grounds were all but deserted, it being far too early for the *ton* to begin its daily promenade. After they circled the entire park twice, Justin ordered the coachman to halt, then helped the ladies alight.

Although the sun was shining, there was a hint of frost in the air. With a faint smile, Annabel inhaled. The breath she drew in contained a trace of bonfire and glancing about she saw piles of crisp leaves waiting to be set afire. Autumn, she mused, had ever been her favorite season, because the fallen leaves made such a satisfying crunch when trod upon.

"I thought it might be pleasant to stroll alongside the Serpentine. Does the idea appeal?"

"It's a splendid notion!" Fanny enthused.

Justin shifted his gaze to Annabel. "And you, Miss Drummond, are you agreeable?"

Egged on by the thought of wading through piles of leaves, Annabel gave her parasol a playful twirl. "Yes, my lord."

"Excellent!"

The earl set off with a fashionably-dressed female on each arm.

Leisurely strolls ranked high on Annabel's list of favorite pastimes. But while she enjoyed taking the air, her sensitivity to Justin's most casual touch set off alarm bells. To be sure, there was nothing improper about taking a gentleman's arm. It was just that she found her total awareness of him unsettling, especially as none of her previous suitors had heated her blood like he did.

In her bemused state, it was not until he'd assisted her back into the landau and let go of her hand in order to perform the same courtesy for Fanny, that Annabel managed to establish a measure of control over her racing pulses.

Twenty minutes later, the hired coachman delivered the trio to Gunter's at number seven Berkeley Square. Annabel's exquisite torment recurred when the earl handed her down from the landau and, tucking her arm in his, led her inside.

Justin seated her in one of the four chairs grouped round a square table swathed in snowy linen. The instant he severed physical contact, Annabel once again felt cut adrift. At pains to conceal hurt feelings, she glanced about the room in search of a respite from sensations which continued to cut up her peace.

Her chair faced a huge arched window, inset with a series of square glass panes and embellished with twin sidelights. Filtered through the glass, sunlight flooded the entire room, creating a cheerful ambience, reinforced by apple green walls and ivory cornices that framed both doors and windows. At a table near to hers, four children ate ices under the watchful eye of their stern-faced nurse.

The youngsters evoked a bitter-sweet memory of her own childhood excursion to Gunter's. Annabel had clung to her mother's hand, too shy to meet Grandmama's gaze.

The poignant scene continued to unfold in mind's eye. Annabel smacked her lips. How delicious the ice melting slowly on her tongue had tasted. How proud dearest Mama had been of her daughter because she hadn't spilt any of it on her frock. She wrinkled her nose. She could still recollect the heady whiff of lilac scent she'd breathed in when Lady Winthrop kissed her goodbye.

Annabel grimaced. Mama died that winter. Visits with her grandmother ceased. She was never able to coax Papa into taking her to Gunter's, so visits to the famed confectioner's had ended. Until today, she'd never been back. And now that she was, she harbored mixed feelings as to the wisdom of confronting child-hood ghosts she thought long since put to rest.

The arrival of a waitress wearing a perky white cap and a black bombazine gown covered by a frilly white apron pulled Annabel back to the present.

"Do you want ices?" the earl asked.

"Ices by all means," Fanny stated firmly.

"What flavor?"

Annabel cleared her throat. "Raspberry, please."

"And I'll have pineapple," said Fanny.

Justin relayed their choices to the waitress and or-dered a strawberry ice for himself. The instant she withdrew, a cavalry officer he'd last seen at Waterloo replaced her.

"Justin! As I live and breath!"

Rising, Justin joined in the mutual back slapping con-test resorted to by veteran campaigners who meet purely by chance. "Adam, it is good to see you looking so fit."

"God's truth! Never thought to see either of us run-ning tame at Gunter's of all places. Just finished treat-ing my brat of a nephew to an ice and packed him off home with his nurse. What's your excuse?"

Justin grinned. "My dear fellow, this is my old stomp-ing grounds, dating back to nursery days, long before I took up soldiering."

Adam gave an impatient swipe at his fine-textured blond hair. Its tendency to hang in his eyes gave him a boyish appearance. It was difficult to believe he al-ready had thirty-five years in his dish.

"I've a bone to pick with you, Major."

Justin lifted an eyebrow. "Do you? I cannot imagine why?"

Captain Worden's serious mien was betrayed by the laughter in his eyes. "See here, old chap. Hardly seems fair that you get to entertain the two most beautiful ladies in the entire room, whilst I cannot even find a spare table."

Justin coolly buffed his fingernails on the lapel of his coat, then examined them with feigned interest. "Indeed, I am the most fortunate of men."

Adam gazed longingly at their table's empty chair before he cast Justin a speaking look. When the earl still failed to take the hint, he resorted to sarcasm. "Well, if you refuse to share the ladies, the least you could do is offer a brother officer a chair to fling his weary bones upon."

His hang-dog expression won a shout of laughter from Justin. "I suppose I'm obliged to offer it, if only for old time's sake."

Adam glared at him. "Your generosity threatens to unman me."

"By all means join us, old chap. Only don't sit down just yet. First, allow me to make you known to the ladies, whom I fear I've neglected far too long."

Justin shifted his gaze to his companions. "Ladies, this scamp is Captain Worden, the consummate cavalry officer." Casting his friend a shrewd glance, he said, "Adam, it is my distinct pleasure to present Miss Drummond."

"Enchanted, fair lady."

"And her companion, Miss Bolton."

Adam swept his fine-textured blond hair from his eyes, then stared at Fanny, clearly dumbstruck.

As the tense silence lengthened, Justin bounced his gaze back and forth between Adam to Fanny. Still puzzled, he shot a questioning glance at Annabel. Her slight shrug indicated she was equally in the dark.

Captain Worden quirked an eyebrow. "Fanny?"

Fanny released a shaky sigh. "How are you, Lord Adam?"

"Fine, thank you. You are more beautiful than I remember." His rueful smile faded. "Sorry about Peter."

"Me, too," said Fanny, her voice a thready whisper.

"Tried to look you up to express my condolences while on furlough. But you'd left your teaching post in Bath and cut your Dorset ties. No one knew where you'd gone."

Noting that Fanny's eyes were abrim with unspilt tears, Annabel said tartly, "The vicar's death left her virtually penniless."

Adam was appalled. "Fanny, I am truly sorry. Had I known I—"

"Have done!" Fanny cried. "The last thing I want or desire is your pity."

"Deuce take it! Ain't hawking pity. Dashed proud of how well you've coped."

"Truly?"

"My dear Fanny, your price is above rubies."

Fanny reacted to the mischievous glimmer in his eyes with an unladylike snort. "Doing it up to brown, my lord."

He cast her a tremulous smile. "So are you, brat. Well you know, I'm not one to stand on ceremony."

A slow tentative smile lit Fanny's face, giving it a kind of soulful beauty that literally took Annabel's breath away. Her gaze shifted to Captain Worden's rather sharp features just in time to see the anxious look in his eyes fade. Annabel blinked, rapidly trying to dislodge the premonition that took root in her mind and stubbornly refused to be banished.

Annabel did not believe in love at first sight. Yet gazing at Adam and Fanny, how else could she account for the tender emotion she saw flowing in both directions?

Seventeen

At Covent Garden, the curtain descended upon the last act of Hamlet. As the steady buzz of low-keyed conversations resumed, Annabel slowly emerged from her trance to find Fanny already on her feet with her arm tucked into Captain Worden's.

"Lord Adam and I fancy a stroll. Do you care to join us, Annabel?"

Annabel gazed at Fanny thoughtfully. Although she did not doubt for a minute that her invitation was sincerely meant, she sensed Fanny craved a private moment with the daring cavalry officer and didn't wish to intrude.

"No thanks. I'm content to stay put."

Captain Worden turned to the last member of the foursome. "What about you, Justin? Care to join me in a mad dash for the lemonade?"

Justin regarded him lazily through hooded eyes. Adam was too deuced impulsive for his own good. But then, overenthusiasm was the bane of all cavalry officers.

"Justin?"

He shook his head. "It is your turn to fetch the lemonade. I'll keep Miss Drummond company."

Obviously eager to have Fanny all to himself, the captain bustled his prize from the box with such unseemly haste that Justin had difficulty holding back a chuckle until the couple were safely out of earshot.

"Gracious! How can you laugh after watching such a gloomy play?" Annabel asked.

Justin awarded her a devil-may-care grin that made mincemeat of her resolve to keep him at arm's length emotionally. It was silly of her to worry about Fanny's welfare when her own seemed in worse jeopardy, Annabel mused. Although she took great pride in her independence, she ached to be enfolded in Justin's strong arms and shielded from worldly cares. And this longing which she seemed to have no control over made her feel vulnerable.

"I prefer laughter to tears. Besides, what else can you expect from Hamlet but gloom and doom?"

"Very true. Mr. Young was very good in the part. Do you not agree?"

"He's certainly no Kemble or Kean, but he'll do."

Annabel glanced at Justin surreptitiously. How she wished she was less aware of his masculine allure. But she mustn't dwell on these treacherous feelings. If she knew what was good for her, she'd do her best to curb them.

"But enough of the moody Danish prince. Patience, my sweet," Justin counseled in that deep voice of his that never failed to riffle the downy hairs at the nape of her neck. "The farce that follows the interval is sure to cheer you up."

Annabel sighed. "I wish I was as certain of that as you seem to be."

She lapsed into a brown study. Papa had thought plays were the work of the devil and had refused to take her. Nor could she and Fanny attend without a male escort to lend them countenance. So tonight was a rare treat, and it was good of Captain Worden to obtain permission from his father to use the ducal box.

Annabel emerged from her daydream to find Justin peering at her intently. "Is something amiss?" she asked.

"You've been in the doldrums all evening. Care to share your troubles?"

Good heavens! Was she really that transparent? she wondered. "No thanks. I wouldn't dream of imposing."

"Gammon! I'll warrant it's Adam and Fanny smelling of April and May that's overset you. Right?"

"To tell the truth, I'm more confused than envious. The loss of her betrothed in a naval engagement devastated Fanny. I assumed she'd rather remain a spinster than risk having her heart broken once again. Obviously, I was wrong."

"Surely the circumstances differ. With England at peace there's little risk Adam will be killed."

"Good point," Annabel conceded stiffly. "I can only hope he's not trifling with her affections."

"I doubt that's his intent. Having survived Waterloo, I expect he'd like to settle down with a wife and raise a family."

"I'd feel better about this whirlwind courtship if I knew more about his prospects."

"I can vouch for his character, but know next to nothing in that regard. I believe his mother left him a snug little estate in Dorset in her will. Which is fortunate because Adam is the youngest of four sons, and of course, the bulk of his grace's estate will pass to Lord Ashford, who is heir to the dukedom."

"Well, at least Fanny won't starve if they marry. But it is early days yet. Perhaps their sentiments will change."

"And save you the bother of hiring another companion?" asked Justin, his demeanor sardonic. "That's what you wish, is it not?"

"I'm not quite so shallow as you seem to think, my

lord. I truly wish Fanny every happiness, even if she chooses marriage over spinsterhood, though I cannot imagine why any sane woman would."

"You are the oddest female. Most women jump at the chance to marry."

"I've nothing against marriage. For others, that is. For myself, I'm content to remain a spinster."

Justin raised an eyebrow. "Matrimony doesn't interest you at all?"

Annabel slowly shook her head. She felt beleaguered and wished she'd chosen to take a stroll during the interval, instead of remaining behind in the hope of assuaging her doubts in regard to Captain Worden's intentions, and if honorable, whether his expectations were sufficient to support a wife. Culling such details had proved awkward. But Fanny didn't have a father or uncle or brother to look out for her best interests. Thus, the unsavory task had fallen squarely on Annabel's shoulders.

"Frankly, I find your antipathy toward marriage passing strange," Justin confessed.

Annabel's control snapped. "Strange am I? Should I be so foolish as to marry, I'd be required to turn my fortune over to my husband to squander as he sees fit. To marry is to surrender my independence. To me, such a sacrifice is too great."

Justin responded with a sardonic chuckle that chilled to the bone. His eyes were flat and cold. Annabel's heart sank. Her candor had given him a disgust of her.

Before the widening chasm grew too uncomfortable, Fanny and Adam reappeared with their lemonade. These days, Fanny possessed an ethereal glow that seemed to emanate from her very soul, Annabel reflected.

Nothing for it. She must let Fanny go. She deserved to be happy and obviously her happiness was inextricably entwined with that of Captain Worden's. Annabel's dark blue eyes grew stormy. But by jingo, he'd best cherish the treasure he'd won else he'd answer to Annabel.

The lights dimmed and the farce entitled *The Maid and the Magpie* began. A Miss Booth was cast in the role of Annette. While the ingenue was comely and her delivery was sprightly, Annabel was too unhappy to notice.

Even more unsettling were her mixed reactions to the present Earl of Summerfield's probes. After all, the last thing she wanted was to marry, was it not? So why did she feel like bursting into tears merely because she'd managed to make her position clear to him?

Justin was right about one thing though. Life was passing strange. Especially when she had reason to suspect she didn't really know her own mind. Or should that be her true sentiments?

Justin peered into his shaving table mirror and groaned. Shoulders slumped, he made a few minor adjustments to his lightly starched cravat under the gimlet-eyed scrutiny of Jamie MacTavish, his former batman.

Although he pretended not to notice MacTavish's fierce stare, Justin was surprised that the looking glass didn't shatter from the sheer force of the Scotsman's scowl. Clearly something was sticking in MacTavish's craw, but Justin would be damned if he'd ask what had put the man in such a pet.

Justin had enough troubles of his own to worry about. For one thing, he had a terrible hangover, which he supposed served him right for drinking blue ruin in the small hours of the night. But damn her eyes, his conversation with Annabel during the interval at Covent Garden had left him blue-deviled.

He stared at his reflection. The bags under his eyes

confirmed he'd slept poorly. Little wonder. From the start of his siege on Annabel's heart, he'd known she wasn't all that keen about marriage. Yet, fool that he was, he'd flattered himself that all he need do was exert a little charm and she'd fall into his arms like a ripe plum.

He gave a mirthless laugh. Nothing could be further from the truth. Scrope Davies was right. The woman was a curst ice maiden. And, more likely than not, he was wasting his time courting her.

Turning from the mirror, the earl fixed his gaze upon MacTavish. During the first siege of Badajoz, MacTavish had shielded him from an enemy barrage with his own body. Later, Justin visited him in the field hospital where he was recovering from a minor wound to ask him to be his batman.

From that day on, Justin never had to worry where his next meal was coming from or where he'd rest his weary head. The wily Scotsman had never failed to contrive a decent meal and a dry bed, regardless of how primitive the terrain or how fierce a battle they happened to be waging.

At war's end, he hadn't had the heart to turn his batman out in the cold, when so many former soldiers couldn't find work. He'd asked MacTavish to stay on as his valet. And while he'd be the first to admit that the foot soldier didn't always know his place, Justin felt they rubbed along well enough together.

Justin smiled at MacTavish. "Well, Jamie, do I pass muster?"

"Och. Ye be tricked oot like a regular town beau. Going awooing agin, are ye?"

He started to shake his head, but the action made him dizzy so he stopped. "Not today. I'm meeting Captain Worden at the White Horse Cellar."

"Weel, 'afor ye shab off, there be a wee problem wi' Sergeant Black."

"Bloody hell!" Justin stormed. "I ought never have let you talk me into such a wild scheme."

The scheme he alluded to had been born the day he'd mentioned to MacTavish how it tore at his guts to see so many cashiered soldiers reduced to beggars. Quicker than hell could scorch a feather, MacTavish had urged him to hire a bunch of the ragged wretches to help put the Rye estate in order. When Justin protested he couldn't afford to, his valet said the men would be glad to work in exchange for bed and board.

His pale blue eyes grew petulant. Before agreeing to ship a wagon-load of veterans to his country estate, he'd made MacTavish promise to oversee the move and not plague him with day-to-day details.

Yet here was MacTavish as bold as brass about to make additional demands. The man was a bloody nuisance! Still, Justin couldn't bring himself to turn his back on him. Not after the feisty Scotsman had saved his sanity more times than he cared to count. And his hide too, for that matter.

"What precisely is Sergeant Black's problem?" asked Justin.

"The mon has a wife and a couple o' wee bairns. He won't leave them stranded."

Justin released a great sigh. "Can't say I blame him. Tell him he may bring his family."

MacTavish beamed him a smile. "I'll tell him, laird."

"If that's all, I'm off."

"Weel, now that ye mention it, there's another wee hitch."

"Really?" Justin regarded his valet with a raised eyebrow meant to intimidate, but which he suspected fell short of the mark. "Pray don't keep me in suspense."

"Weel, Major, if ye allow the sergeant's brood, it

dinna seem fair not to let Corporal Woodruff bring along his wife and bairns, too."

Hoodwinked, by God! Justin admitted glumly. "Why not," he agreed with barely-contained fury. "The more the merrier, say I!"

When the wily Scotsman had the wisdom to keep his tongue between his teeth, the earl eyed him sardonically.

"A word of warning, MacTavish. Should I end up in the poorhouse as a result of your grandiose scheme, I plan to drag you along with me."

MacTavish cast him a sweet smile. "I dinna doot it. Who else'd see ta yer welfare?"

Struck momentarily speechless, but unwilling to let his cheeky valet have the last word, he drawled, "Despite the concoction you insisted I swallow, I still have a devilish headache. So pray don't beat around the bush. Are there any more bombshells you plan to drop?"

"If ye mean more wives and bairns, the answer is no."

Justin rolled his eyes heavenward and exclaimed, "Thank God for small favors!"

Eighteen

The White Horse Cellar was one of several coaching inns located on Piccadilly. As usual, it was bursting at the seams with transits either arriving or leaving town. While the place was packed, Justin knew he was in luck when Adam hailed him from a table he'd managed to commandeer. Headed toward it, he narrowly escaped being run down by a sea of passengers, who'd just filed out of The Rocket, eager for a hot meal.

Once the mob thundered past, a shaken Justin staggered over to Adam's table and collapsed into a chair. A waiter slapped a bowl of oyster stew in front of him and another in front of Captain Worden, then departed.

"What the devil?"

Adam cast him an unrepentant grin. "Food's great, but service's abysmal. Trust you like oysters."

Justin's taste buds watered. Sensing the hardy stew would be the very thing to settle his queasy stomach, he flashed Adam a smile.

"My dear chap, I dote on them."

"Splendid!"

Justin savored a chewy spoonful. To be sure, he mused, it was presumptuous of Adam to order for him, yet he was glad Adam had. Last night's drinking bout had curdled Justin's innards, but now that he was feeling more the thing, he realized he was hungry.

"Next comes lamb cutlets served with cauliflower and dressed dandelion. Dessert is apple fritters."

"Excellent! However did you guess I'm dashed peckish?"

Adam snorted. "Half-starved more like! But tell me, what has you down in the hips?"

Justin sighed. "I fear the lady doesn't fancy becoming a wife. Or at least, not *my* wife."

"According to Fanny, Miss Drummond has an aversion to marriage."

"I've come to the same painful conclusion. For tuppence I'd throw in the towel."

"What? Give up so soon? Only been courting her a few weeks. Surely such a prize's worth more time and more patience."

"That's the crux of my problem. I'm fast running out of both. Camden Manor is in dire need of a new roof."

"So go fix the bloody roof and pick up where you left off afterward."

Justin winced. "Do me a favor, Adam, and lower your curst voice."

"Sorry, old chap."

"Forget it. As to your suggestion, I'm not sure I've the courage to launch yet another siege on my lady's heart."

"The devil you say! Just because you've suffered a setback? Shame on you. Only think how many times we lost and regained the same dashed towns during the Peninsula Campaign. Defeat only comes when and if you give up."

"It is easy for you to take that road. Fanny's in love with you. She'd make you an excellent wife—provided of course marriage is your intention."

Adam glared at him. "Of course, my intentions are honorable. Only reason I'm dragging my feet is lack of a place to live until next spring when the lease to the property my mother left me runs out. Not that his grace would refuse us house room. My father is dashed proud of me, if I say so myself," Adam averred.

"With good reason," Justin agreed, recalling that Adam had been cited more than once for bravery under fire in the dispatches.

"Nor do I doubt for a minute that he'll dote on Fanny once he gets to know her. He'd be happy to put us up 'til spring, but I find the family mausoleum in Kent dashed depressing. Don't fancy spending our honeymoon there."

"No, I can see you don't. But how is it that his grace doesn't know Fanny? I thought her father was the local vicar."

"So he was. My father knew of her existence, of course, since he and her father were on good terms. But Fanny was only three when my mother died. Afterward, his grace never set foot in Dorset again. I guess the place reminded him of her and he couldn't bear the pain."

Justin nodded. "A distinct possibility."

"Quite," said Adam. "I, on the other hand, loved the place and spent all my summers there. Peter Shaw was the son of the local squire. He and I were bosom bows. Fanny was such a taking minx, we let her tag along."

"Well, if a place to stay is the only drawback, it's easily solved."

"Is it?"

"Of a certainty! There's a snug little cottage on my estate, that's in good repair. You're welcome to live there with your bride until your own property is available."

"Bloody generous of you, old stick. But really, I couldn't impose."

"Fustian! I'm happy to offer the place rent free, but

if it will assuage your pride, you can repay me by helping me whip Camden Manor into some sort of reason-
able shape. After all, should I get lucky and persuade
my reluctant heiress to wed me, I don't want to give
her a disgust of the family pile right off."

"Excellent point. As for your offer, I'll bear it in mind
when I pop the question."

"You mean to pay your addresses soon, do you?"

Adam nodded. "Thirty-five years in my dish. High
time I set up my nursery."

"And you think Fanny will agree to marry you?"

"Yes." Adam swept his fine-textured blond hair off
his forehead, exposing a faint frown. "Only obstacle is
Miss Drummond. Fanny is very conscientious. Depend
upon it! She'll refuse to leave her in the lurch."

"I doubt Annabel will stand in the way of her friend's
happiness."

"Indeed, I pin my hopes on her generosity. But
enough of my plans. Shall we put our heads together
to see if we can get your courtship back on course?"

"My dear fellow, I'd be most appreciative of any advice you care to offer."

"Excellent. First off, tell me what's your main stum-
bling block?"

Justin thought wistfully of the only time he'd ever
managed to slip past her defenses and kiss her. That
kiss had forged a bond between them. And the memory
of her melting into him during that tender caress had
sustained him through many a battle. Still, two years
was a devilish long time between kisses.

"Ah, that's easy! Other than helping her in and out
of carriages or offering her my arm, I've no excuse to
touch her. It is a great pity she shuns society. Were she
part of the social whirl, I could ask her to dance. I
might even get lucky and manage to steal a kiss or two.
But as things stand, I've no chance to draw close

enough to melt her resistance, no chance to woo her properly."

Adam's fine hair was hanging in his eyes once again. He made short work of brushing it aside. "Got a brainstorm. Will ask Fanny to marry me immediately. Once she agrees, my father will insist upon giving a ball to announce our betrothal. Naturally, Fanny will wish her best friend be present. Frankly, old chap, I don't see how Miss Drummond can refuse to attend."

A knowing smile spread slowly across Justin's handsome features. "By God, that's the ticket!"

Adam's grin stretched from ear to ear. "Good thing you had the foresight to invite me to join your table at Gunter's. Without me, your courtship would surely have foundered."

Still smiling, Justin genially invited Captain Worden to put a sock to it.

If she peered at those same figures much longer she'd end up cross-eyed, Annabel thought as she pushed the ledger aside.

Her dark blue eyes scanned the room that had once been her father's study. After his death, she'd consigned the heavy mahogany furniture he'd favored to the attic and substituted less cumbersome pieces, whose cleaner lines and absence of rococo flourishes were more to her taste.

Her lips pursed. Outside, the fog was thick enough to cut with a knife. She doubted the gloomy weather was the reason she felt out of curl. She blamed her dampened spirits on Justin. He had not called on her for a sennight. And much as it aggravated her to admit it, she missed him sorely.

"Ahem!"

Glancing toward the open doorway, Annabel exclaimed, "Gracious me, Fanny! Quit peeking round the door jamb. Show yourself and have done."

Clearly flustered, Fanny stepped across the threshold. "I . . . that is, we need to speak to you. Is this a convenient time or shall we come back later?"

Annabel gazed at her companion thoughtfully. Never had she seen Fanny so nervous. Something was definitely afoot. Her gazed narrowed. So good of Fanny to drop her a hint.

"We?" she queried softly.

Fanny gave a nervous giggle and glanced back over her shoulder. "Yes, we. Adam and I wish to . . ."

Captain Adam Worden emerged from the shadows. He boldly placed his hand on Fanny's waist and pulled her close to his side. Smiling down at her, he announced firmly, "Fanny and I wish to speak to you about our future plans."

This was it, thought Annabel. *She was actually going to lose her companion.* The realization invoked a sick feeling in the pit of her stomach.

Nevertheless, it was beneath her dignity to be rude. She pushed her chair away from the library table and rose to her feet. Moving with grace, she saw the couple comfortably settled upon an empire sofa upholstered in azure silk brocade before she retired to a nearby wing chair. Only then, did she trust her voice not to quaver as she begged them to open their budgets.

Adam and Fanny exchanged a besotted look that wrung Annabel's heartstrings, but the only outward indication of her grief was the slight tightening of her mouth.

"I am the happiest of men. Miss Bolton has agreed to become my wife."

The captain's words reverberated in Annabel's ears until she wanted to scream. They rang like a death knell to her close friendship with Fanny. It wouldn't be so bad if Annabel made friends easily. But she didn't. Besides, Fanny was irreplaceable.

"Dearest, I cannot bear for you to mope on the happiest day of my life. Just because I'm getting married, doesn't mean I shan't always treasure our friendship."

"Your sentiments do you credit. But gracious me, how I shall miss you!"

Fanny shot her a plea for her understanding. "I shan't totally desert you. We can pay each other visits."

"Yes, of course, we can," she concurred briskly.

That the lovebirds hadn't taken her into their confidence earlier hurt Annabel. Not only did she feel abandoned, she felt betrayed. Why hadn't Fanny told her sooner? It was not like her to be so secretive.

With a stiff, brittle smile, Annabel tossed down the gauntlet. "Where do you plan to live? Kent?"

Fanny and Adam exchanged another of those looks that touched Annabel on the raw. Then, seemingly by mutual agreement, the captain elected to respond.

"Lord, no. Not that his grace would mind putting us up for as long as we cared to stay. My father is the soul of generosity, if I say so myself. But the mouldering castle has been in the family since the Norman invasion and is dashed drafty. I don't fancy my bride catching pneumonia on our honeymoon."

"Most considerate. But if not the family castle, where do you plan to set up housekeeping?"

"My mother left me a snug property in Dorset. Fanny and I plan to settle there . . . eventually."

"You intend to pursue your army career first, do you?"

Adam shook his head. "With Boney in exile, army life will be a dead bore. No change of advancement to look forward to either. Besides, Fanny is too delicate to follow the drum. Far better that we settle in Dorset where she can look after our nursery, whilst I raise thoroughbreds. The problem is we cannot take possession until next spring when the present lease expires."

"Then you plan a lengthy engagement?"

The captain nodded. "So, you see, I don't intend to steal away your lovely companion immediately. You'll have plenty of time to find another."

"And Fanny will have time to see to her trousseau."

"So she will," he agreed.

She cast him a pensive look. What a relief that he planned to sell his commission. She shuddered to think how Fanny might have fared had Lord Adam elected to stay in the army. Had his regiment been assigned to India, the likelihood that she'd ever set eyes on Fanny again was decidedly slim.

Thus, while disheartened over losing Fanny, she had to give Captain Worden credit. His plans for the future seemed sensible. However, there were other reservations that must be broached before Annabel could feel entirely easy about Fanny's betrothal.

Before she could decide how best to couch her concerns, Fanny thrust her left hand forward, and said, "How remiss of me not to show you my betrothal ring? Isn't it beautiful?"

Annabel stared at the pear-shaped diamond, awestruck. "Truly it's exquisite." She addressed her next remark to Adam. "An heirloom?"

He shook his head. "After I took Fanny to call at the family digs on Henrietta Street and received my father's blessings, I spirited her off to Rundell and Bridges and let her have the pick of the lot."

Annabel regarded him with skepticism. "How very generous of you to be sure. But are you certain you can afford—"

Cheeks burning, she broke off in mid-sentence: "Dear me. How unpardonably rude of me. Pray disregard it."

Clearly amused by her discomfiture, Adam gave vent to a hearty laugh. Annabel resented that. However, what really ruffled her feathers was knowing she couldn't risk giving him the setdown he richly deserved—not without alienating Fanny.

Sobering, Adam set about making amends. "I beg your pardon, Miss Drummond. I confess your assumption that Fanny's ring will drive us to the poorhouse tickled my funnybone. I trust it will relieve your mind to know that during my years on the Peninsula my father made me a very generous allowance. Having little occasion to spend it between battles, I squirreled away a considerable nest egg as a hedge against unforeseen expenses."

Annabel shot him a grateful smile. "I appreciate your frankness. I am sure it's none of my business, but I shall sleep better nights knowing she'll never be in want."

"Mind you," he cautioned, "I ain't exactly rolling in wealth. While my father's as rich as a nabob, the bulk of his estate will pass to my eldest brother. And of course, my brothers Robert and Edward have to be provided for as well. But I do not repine. I'm a dab hand with horses, and am confident I can adequately provide for a wife and family."

"Enough, sir. You've convinced me she'll be in good hands. I believe I'll ask Fenton to fetch a bottle of champagne from the cellar. We must toast your betrothal."

Nineteen

Later that same evening Annabel looked back over the day. Somehow she'd managed to maintain an outer facade of bubbly cheerfulness. Somehow she'd carried off the impromptu celebration of Fanny's betrotha without a hitch. She'd let Fanny prattle on and on all evening without a murmur of protest. And although the champagne Annabel had drunk gave her a blinding headache, she hadn't uttered a single cross word.

She'd just kept on smiling like a demented ninny hammer until she feared her face would crack. Never mind that she was about to lose Fanny. Never mind that no companion she might hire would ever suit her as well. It wouldn't be fair to pressure Fanny not to marry simply because Annabel had grave reservations in regard to the institution.

To be candid, ever since Captain Adam Worden had stepped into their lives at Gunter's, Fanny positively glowed. Annabel never doubted they loved each other. In short, it was a marriage made in heaven. It would be spiteful to raise the slightest objection. Not to mention sour grapes.

However, she did wish Fanny hadn't asked her to be her bridesmaid. She hated to be the cynosure of all eyes. It was too reminiscent by far of the time she'd been jilted at the altar. But, in common with Annabel Fanny did not have very many friends, so how could

Annabel possibly refuse? The answer was, she couldn't. Friends did not let each other down.

Just the same, Annabel was adamant about not attending Fanny's betrothal ball. The Duke of Skye was hosting the affair at his mansion in Henrietta Street. It would be good for Fanny to begin to grow accustomed to rubbing shoulders with the *ton*. But Annabel needn't be present. Fanny would be all right. Lord Adam would look after her.

Nor need Annabel feel guilty. She was not the bride. There was no need for her to go. No need for her to mingle with the *ton*.

Another reason for staying away was that Justin would probably attend. While it hurt that he no longer called on her, that pain was neglible in comparison to what she'd suffer if she caught him flirting with another woman.

Besides, hardheaded businesswomen did not behave like social butterflies. And, much as she hated to disappoint Fanny, Annabel felt she must draw the line somewhere.

A fortnight later, Justin returned to London from Camden Manor, invigorated by what firm resolve combined with elbow grease had accomplished at his country estate. The wagon-load of foot soldiers he'd escorted to Sussex had pitched in eagerly. Some helped the roofers lay slabs of slate on the mansion's roof; some pruned deadwood in the apple orchard; some planted a vegetable garden and weeded the herb bed. The rest formed a work crew to make repairs to the cottages.

Nor had the inclusion of soldiers' families been the burden he'd anticipated. Indeed, as soon as the two soldiers' wives had settled in, they'd taken turns sending his supper in a covered dish, saving him the expense

of hiring a cook. In hindsight, he'd admitted he ough
to have realized that women who followed their drum
were hardy souls used to making the best of things.

As for Justin himself, when he wasn't laboring along
side his men, he'd divided his time between overseering
each project, meeting with his tenants, and drawing up
plans for a new stable to replace the ramshackle affair
that was clearly on its last legs.

Nevertheless, even on the days when he engaged in
hard physical labor from dawn to dusk, he yearned for
his chosen bride. Indeed, it would be fair to say he'd
become obsessed with winning Annabel's stubborn
heart. He wanted to wake each morning and find her
in his bed. He wanted to be able to reach out and touch
her. And yes, he wanted to plant a child in her belly.
But, most of all, he wanted to have the right to cherish
her.

The hours between midnight and dawn were the
worst times, Justin conceded. Night after night he'd
fallen in bed physically exhausted—only to wake hours
before dawn. Night after night, he'd lain there in a cold
sweat, pining for her sweet body. Night after night, he'd
tried to think of an honorable way to melt Annabel's
resistance to marriage.

His torment had ended with the arrival of an invitation to Adam and Fanny's betrothal ball. Unable to pass
up this chance to woo Annabel in a romantic setting,
Justin had left MacTavish in charge and hied to London, determined to make one more assault on his beloved's cold heart.

But while Justin was eager to attend the betrothal
ball, Annabel refused to let Fanny coax her into coming.
Ever strong-willed, she held firm to her resolve until

the following Tuesday at Hatchard's where, quite by chance, on her part at least, she ran into Justin.

He doffed his hat and cast her an admiring glance that did wonders for her flagging spirits. "My dear, Miss Drummond, what a fetching bonnet."

Her French chapeau of green moss silk was adorned with a single plume of white feathers. She'd tied its green and white plaid ribbons in a secure bow under her chin.

"Thank you, my lord."

Annabel tried to brush aside his compliment and remain level-headed. It was as if he'd touched her wherever he looked. Well not exactly, she amended. It was as if he were savouring her with his eyes instead of his tongue.

" It is not every day one runs into a vision in a bookshop."

"Pigswill!"

"Little termagant," he crooned tenderly. "How I missed your setdowns whilst stuck in Sussex."

"Sussex?"

He nodded. "My estate is there."

Annabel felt as if a load of bricks had suddenly been lifted from her shoulders. She'd feared he had been ignoring her because he'd formed a disgust of her. But such was not the case. He'd merely been out of town.

"I've been rusticating there for the past fortnight."

Annabel raised an eyebrow. "In trouble with the dunsters, my lord?"

"Minx! Much as I hate to disappoint you, I am neither a gamester nor a spendthrift. I went to supervise the raising of the new slate roof needed to protect Camden Manor from further deterioration."

"Oh? Did you sell your town house?"

He shook his head, his gaze enigmatic. "I reluctantly parted with a priceless Canaletto an ancestor dragged home from Venice a century past."

"You sound very pleased with yourself?"

He grinned. "So I am. The family motto is We Shall Contrive."

"Are you aware that during your absence Miss Bolton and Lord Adam became betrothed?"

"Yes, I read the announcement in the morning paper. As a matter of fact, when I called on Adam to inform him of my return, he asked me to have a word with you about that very matter."

"He has?"

Justin nodded. "He hopes I can persuade you to change your mind and come to the ball."

Annabel bristled. "It will do no good to badger me. I don't care for society and see no reason to attend."

"You don't consider Fanny's peace of mind sufficient reason?"

"It is Captain Worden's place to look after her," she insisted.

"Certainly he'll try. But should he be diverted, the biddies will tear her to shreds."

"Nonsense! His family will rally round her. Fanny told me herself that his grace seems fond of her."

"I'm sure he is. However, his grace has a weakness for cards. I'll wager as soon as the ball begins, he'll make a beeline for the whist table.

"Furthermore, the duke's heir, Lord Ashford is too high in the instep to take much notice of a mere vicar's daughter. His wife, Lady Ashford, is an even worse snob. Adam's other two brothers are selfish fribbles, too lazy to intercede on her behalf. Naturally, I'll help Adam shield her all I can. We'll do everything in our power to see that Miss Bolton is left with a happy memory of her betrothal ball. But without you there to play duenna, there are no guarantees."

Ashen-faced, Annabel glared up at her tormentor. "I

don't have to listen to this." With an anguished cry, she clamped her hands over her ears.

His expression grim, Justin darted a quick glance about the bookshop. Then, apparently reassured no one had heard her outcry, he hustled her into a dim alcove where they'd be less conspicuous. There, he pried her hands off her ears.

"Oh, no you don't, little coward. I must insist you hear me out," he muttered through clenched teeth.

One glimpse into his icy blue eyes convinced her it would be folly to anger him further.

"Very well, I shall listen to what you have to say. But first loosen your grip before you snap my wrists in two."

Justin's hands dropped away. Her wrists throbbed painfully as circulation improved, but she made no complaint. Intent upon extricating herself from this coil as swiftly as possible, Annabel cast him a haughty stare.

"Do continue, my lord."

"As you wish. Adam and I cannot be everywhere. Even if she gains family support, there is only one female amongst them. Unless you acquiesce, Miss Bolton will be virtually friendless on the feminine side of the ledger. The first time she retires to the ladies' cloakroom, the vicious hags will pounce. Neither Adam nor I can prevent them from cutting up her peace. Is that the fate you wish for your bosom bow?"

"No, of course not."

The realization that her attitude was both wrongheaded and self-serving was painful. Truth be told, the possible repercussions of her decision to shun Fanny's betrothal ball hadn't occurred to her. But now that Justin had etched them in acid, she felt honor bound to attend for Fanny's sake, even though she suspected she'd have a miserable time.

"Very well, you've convinced me. You may be sure I'll be there to keep an eye on Fanny."

The rigid set of Justin's shoulders eased. "Miss Bolton is fortunate to have you as a friend."

"No more fortunate than I." Annabel sighed. "Without her counsel, I shall feel rudderless."

"If it's any consolation, Adam will do everything in his power to make her happy."

"Yes, I believe he will. Did I not, I'd have fought him tooth and nail. But Miss Bolton loves him. So, you see, I'd really no choice but to give her my blessings."

Justin issued her a tender smile. "Rest assured you've done the right thing," he said, as he gently tucked a wayward auburn ringlet back inside her stylish bonnet.

Overwhelmed by the brush of his fingers across her cheek, Annabel shivered and took an involuntary step backward. How could she have forgotten what his slightest touch did to her? There were no words to describe the deep yearning it engendered.

Annabel cast her eyes to the heavens. Angels defend her! She was behaving like a besotted ninny. And the sooner she cut short this chance encounter the better!

"My dear Miss Drummond, allow me to steal the march on your many admirers certain to flock to your side the instant you set foot in the ballroom. Mark me down for a waltz and the supper dance on your card."

Justin bowed and sauntered off before she could make up her mind whether or not to grant him this boon. Yet, once she'd had time to think about it, she had to admire the lengths Justin was willing to go to in order to oblige a friend. For Adam's sake, he'd agreed to take on an assignment he probably would have preferred to avoid. For what man in his right mind would willingly approach a prickly spinster unused to having her judgment questioned? The answer Annabel came up with was either a very brave man or a moonling.

Any man who'd served with distinction under Wellington had to be courageous. So, in all fairness, Annabel reluctantly conceded, Justin had earned many times over the privilege of the two dances he'd requested.

Annabel was all set to rap on the bedchamber door when it opened and the abigail she shared with Fanny joined her in the hallway.

"All done?" she asked.

The abigail bobbed her head up and down, then fled. Annabel frowned at her retreating figure. The young servant's skills were top of the trees. If only she could be taught not to skulk about like a startled rabbit.

Annabel gave herself a mental shake. Never mind the abigail. Annabel had other fish to fry. She pinned a smile on her face and entered the bedchamber.

Fanny's carmel-colored tresses had been dressed high and interwoven with pink rosebuds sent by Lord Adam. She caught sight of Annabel in the looking glass and whirled around to face her.

Annabel's breath caught in her throat as she admired the ball gown she'd commissioned after overcoming Fanny's qualms. Its underdress of white glace silk was partially hidden by an overdress of amber silk. The rich color had been an inspired choice. It highlighted the gold flecks in Fanny's brown eyes.

"Such a lovely gown. How can I ever thank you?"

Annabel made a wry face. "Do give over. One more thank you and I may strangle you."

"It is hard to keep mum wearing a gown fit for a princess."

"Here. This is for you." Annabel thrust a small, be-ribboned box into Fanny's startled hands.

"Another gift? Really, I couldn't."

"I declare you put me all out of patience! Open it. They go with your gown."

Fanny glared mutinously at Annabel who countered by thrusting her chin forward.

"It is the merest bauble. I swear if you don't accept it graciously, I *will* strangle you."

Several more eon-weighted seconds wended past before Fanny capitulated. "Very well. But only if you promise to cease showering me with gifts."

"I still don't see why you refused to let me pay for your trousseau," Annabel grumbled.

"Do you promise?"

Annabel raised her right hand as if taking an oath. "I vow to think twice before buying any more baubles. Now for heaven's sake, open the box."

Fanny undid the pink satin bow and raised the lid.

"Oh," she gasped. Her brown eyes brimmed with awe. "They must have cost the earth."

"Fiddle faddle! Semi-precious gems do not cost the earth. Put them on and have done."

Frowning, Fanny attached one polished amber earring and reached for its mate. "You'll spoil me."

Annabel's gaze softened. "Good. You could use a little cosseting."

Twenty

As one of two dozen guests invited to the dinner party preceding the ball, Justin had intended to arrive early enough to observe Annabel's entrance and plan his strategy. But donning evening clothes without Mac-Tavish's aid proved trickier than Justin had envisioned. Clumsy oaf that he was, he felt as if all his fingers had suddenly turned into thumbs.

Justin was still making last minute adjustments to his pristine neckcloth as the landeau turned west on Henrietta Street. Only a few more blocks to travel. With luck, he'd arrived on time. Scant moments later, he saw it was hopeless—thanks to a traffic glut that reduced progress to a standstill. Muttering an oath, Justin heaved himself out of the landeau. He dismissed his carriage and proceeded on foot to the Worden residence located on the corner of Henrietta and Cavendish Square.

Arriving later than he wished, he looked a bit harried as he entered the mansion's drawing room barely in time to escort his assigned dinner partner into the dining room and see her seated beside him at midtable. Glancing about, he was able to catch only an occasional glimpse of Annabel's fiery red hair. That she was placed close to the foot wouldn't have been so bad if she weren't seated on the same side as himself.

Keenly disappointed, he consoled himself that the evening was young, and that later on in the ballroom, he'd have ample chance to press his suit. Meantime, he elected to inventory his fellow guests. At the head of the table, the portly Duke of Skye presided. Lady Jersey's rank entitled her to the seat on his right. As usual, she was jabbering like a magpie. But although his grace showed her every courtesy, he paid more attention to Fanny, whose betrothal to his youngest son had earned her the dubious privilege of being seated to his immediate left. Shy and retiring, she seemed to draw strength from Adam, who flanked her other side. At the opposite end of the table, the duke's daughter-in-law, Lady Ashford, acted as hostess. Justin smiled thinly. A cold fish by all accounts!

His eyes skimmed past a Bedford, a Lamb, a Ponsonby and the young Duke of Devonshire, Hart Spencer. Justin had little trouble deducing that his host was a died-in-the-wool Whig.

Not that he cared a tinker's damn. Whig or Tory, he considered politics a dead bore. A rueful grin surfaced. He needn't have bothered to poll an entire tableful of guests to learn which political party his grace favored. All he need do is train his gaze upon his dinner partner.

He eyed Lady Holland with wary trepidation. Even now, despite forty-five years in her dish, the willful termagant was still beautiful enough to render her present husband's wild behavior two decades ago understandable. Lord Holland had precipitated a raging scandal by stealing the former Lady Webster right out from beneath her first husband's nose. Sir Godfrey Webster had sued for divorce, naming Holland correspondent.

To his credit, Holland had married his mistress the instant she was free. Alas, with the passage of years, Holland's dashing impetuosity had been replaced by an unbecoming meekness that made it difficult to visualize him in the role of reckless seducer.

As for his wife, she'd become renowned as the Whig party's foremost hostess. Justin grinned as his quirky sense of humor kicked into high gear. Never mind that for several years after her divorce and subsequent re-marriage, she was considered to be beyond the pale. Never mind that no lady of virtue dared grace her table for fear of ruining her own reputation. That only the male sex attended her dinner parties never bothered their hostess one whit. Lady Holland made no bones about her preference for the masculine gender as ap-posed to the female.

The vagaries of ever-fickle society coaxed a cynical smile from Justin. Seemingly, the passage of years had dulled the gossipmongers' memories to the point that the furor her divorce had caused was now all but for-gotten. At present, Lady Holland had more invitations to social events than she could shake a stick at, and only a few high-sticklers continued to cut her.

His pale blue eyes brimmed with sardonic amuse-ment. To give my lady her due, at least she'd seen fit to honor her marriage vows the second time round.

The bell-like ring created by tapping a table knife against glass drew all eyes to the head of the table. His grace seemed to have a devil of a time hauling himself upright. But once he'd accomplished the seemingly im-possible feat, he gazed benignly at his assembled guests whilst liveried footmen refilled wineglasses. Only when the footmen retired, did he pointedly clear his throat.

"My youngest son, Lord Adam, served with distinc-tion under Wellington. Now that Boney's wings have been clipped, the dear boy desires to wed this lovely young creature seated beside me. So my lords and ladies and gentlemen, kindly raise your glasses so we may all toast the happy couple."

In the receiving line, Justin kissed Fanny's hand and wished her happy, all the while painfully aware of

Adam's knowing grin. Moving on, Justin shook Adam's hand and congratulated him on his good fortune.

"Knew you'd show up."

Justin burst out laughing. "What an ingrate I'd be if I didn't after all the trouble you've gone to on my behalf."

"Anything for a friend," Adam quipped before turning to greet the next well-wisher in line.

Justin continued to chuckle as he strolled into the ballroom. Adam was a notorious tease. The betrothal ball honoring the engaged couple would have taken place even if Justin had chosen to rusticate.

He sobered. This was no laughing matter. He hoped the romantic backdrop would help his cause. This latest siege to the reluctant heiress's heart must succeed. He couldn't stomach another setback. This was the final roll of the dice. This time he must win.

Justin frowned. Before he could woo Annabel, he must find her. Adam said she'd gone through the reception line earlier, so she had to be there someplace. The question was, where? He scanned the ballroom. No Annabel.

A surge of unadulterated panic tore through him. Surely she hadn't been so shatter-brained as to let herself be lured onto the terrace by some lecher bent on compromising her?

Heart pounding like a kettledrum, he slipped through the French doors. To his immense relief, he found the walled-in terrace entirely deserted, save himself of course. That made perfect sense. After all, it wasn't the dead of summer when the press of too many warm bodies in the ballroom made one covet a breath of fresh air. It was autumn and the night air was nippy.

Swallowing his chagrin, he sidled back inside the ballroom and anxiously scanned the dancers. The ladies' gowns created an ever-changing montage of pastel blurs as their partners whirled them about the dance floor.

Still no sign of Annabel. Drat it!

Justin was about to abandon all hope of finding her in this crush when he sighted her. Although she was on the other side of the dance floor and stood with her back facing him, he'd know those lovely auburn tresses anywhere. A wave of tenderness engulfed him. He loved the stubborn minx to distraction. Whatever would he do if he worked up the nerve to pay his addresses again and she refused him?

He squared his shoulders. Attitude was everything. Only a fool anticipated defeat before the first salvo had been fired. His best course was to cross his fingers and advance.

As he neared, he decided that whoever had designed her gown possessed a rare talent. The back view exposed a tantalizing wedge of alabaster skin that culminated at the small of her back. Her baby soft skin would tempt a saint. His manhood hardened.

Wide panels of exquisite lace were first gathered, then allowed to cascade like a waterfall to the hem of her gown. Navy blue satin ribbands—the exact shade of her remarkable eyes—lent contrast to the pure white concoction, as did her fiery-red locks, gathered at the crown and allowed to tumble in a seemingless artless fashion.

Justin halted in his tracks. His senses were swamped by an almost irresistible compulsion to trail kisses from the nape of her neck all the way down to the small of her back. Yet to do so in public would be sure to percipitate a scandal, which was the last thing he wanted. He truly didn't wish to embarrass her. Gritting his teeth, he closed his eyes and concentrated on keeping a tighter rein on his libido.

Lady Holland's petulant voice drifted into his consciousness. He ignored her chatter in order to concentrate on achieving his first hurdle. He must claim his waltz with Annabel before someone else stole the march on him.

"Miss Drummond, my stripling son fancies himself in love with you. 'Tis calf love of course."

Justin opened his eyes and perked up his ears. Devil a bit! Annabel wasn't up to Lady Holland's weight. If her ladyship decided to bare her claws, he must step in.

"I quite agree," said Annabel quietly.

"See here, Mama, you've no right to interfere," the young man protested.

Lady Holland snorted. "Don't stand there like a block. Make yourself useful. Fetch Miss Drummond and me a glass of punch."

"But Mama, I—"

"Nodcock! Take yourself off before I lose my temper."

Looking every bit as petulant as his mother, the lad stalked off.

Lady Holland refocused her attention on Annabel. "Silly cawker falls in love with a different wench each week. Pray disregard his braying."

"You may be certain I shall, ma'am. Now, if you'll excuse me, I see someone I desire a word with."

Lady Holland's bony fingers seized her wrist, halting her flight. "Not so fast. I haven't had my say."

Annabel yanked her arm free and glared at her oppressor. "Lay a hand on me again and you'll regret it."

Justin's broad chest expanded with pride. He'd been ready to intercede, but Annabel seemed to be holding her own. Lady Holland released an eerie cackle that set his teeth on edge. "Humph! You've got bottom. I admire that. Now then, what's your opinion of the British government's treatment of Boney?"

"Boney, ma'am? I'm unacquainted with any such person."

"Surely you jest. Everyone's heard of the little emperor."

"Ah. You refer to Napoleon Bonaparte, do you not?"

Lady Holland's eyebrows rose to her hairline. "Who else? Do you not agree that the allies have treated the poor man shabbily?"

"I take no interest in politics. Are you sure you want my opinion?"

"Silly chit! I wouldn't ask if I weren't curious."

"Well, since you insist, I think he's gotten his just deserts."

"Rubbish! 'Tis disgraceful to banish him to that barren island. I sent the poor, dear man books to amuse him on his journey to St. Helene. But no one listens to me. Except Byron of course, who has his own troubles to deal with."

Catching Annabel's bedazed look, Justin stepped forward. "Pardon me, Lady Holland, but the young lady has promised me a waltz."

"Ah, Summerfield. Blood up, is it? Never mind. By all means spirit her off whilst I scout out my next victim."

Lady Holland ended her remarks with a cackle calculated to raise the dead. Wincing, Justin offered Annabel his arm. She latched onto it as if it were a lifeline.

Concerned, he glanced at her. Noting her paleness and the haunted look in her dark blue eyes, Justin whisked her from the ballroom into the library and closed the door behind them.

She cast him a suspicious glance. "Why bring me here? I thought you wished to dance."

"I've been looking forward to our waltz since Hatchard's. But our dance can wait. You're far too pale to suit me."

Annabel rolled her eyes. "Who wouldn't be? Is she mad?"

He shook his head. "Merely eccentric."

"Oh?" She mulled this over. "Who is she?"

"Lady Holland. She's what the *ton* refers to as an original."

"Well, that explains it," she said sarcastically. "Here I'd thought I'd been waylaid by a bedlamite!"

Justin snickered. Annabel cast him a look of loathing.

"Lady Holland is not mad," he said firmly.

She shot him an incredulous look. "Really?"

"Yes, really." When Annabel continued to stare at him in disbelief, he deigned it wise to amend his statement. "That is, she is only mad in regard to a single subject."

"Let me see if I understand you, my lord. Do you mean to say her madness is limited to Napoleon Bonaparte?"

"Exactly so! While notoriously eccentric, she only goes queer in the cockloft when that cursed tyrant's name comes up."

"I see. You may be sure I shall take care to never so much as breathe his name in her presence."

"Far better you steer clear of her entirely."

"Excellent advice." Annabel's expression grew pensive. "What do you suppose set her off?"

Justin grinned. "I rather suspect it was his grace's toast to the betrothed couple."

"Why of course! How clever of you, my lord."

Justin basked in the warm approval reflected in her beautiful eyes. He longed to steal a kiss but feared if he did there'd be hell to pay. Much better to leave intact the fragile bridge of trust he'd taken such pains to erect between them.

"Your color is better. Shall we return to the ballroom before we're missed?"

Twenty-one

Annabel heard the maid moving about her bedchamber but continued to play hibernating bear. She wasn't ready to get up yet. She wanted to keep on dreaming.

And such sweet dreams! Her thoughts drifted back to the ball she'd attended last night. She relived the exquisite sensations she'd experienced when she'd let Justin steal a kiss in the library. Well, not steal exactly. The truth was she'd seen his hand on the doorknob and panicked.

Unable to stop herself, she'd blurted, "Aren't you going to kiss me?"

But all that had happened last night. It was now the following morning and the very idea that she'd been so brazen embarrassed her. Little wonder her cheeks burned hotly.

She hazarded a peek through discreetly lowered lashes. The maid knelt on the hearth while she built a fire. The chances of her noticing Annabel's red cheeks were decidedly slim.

More memories bombarded Annabel. Once again she recalled the queasy sensation in the pit of her stomach as she saw Justin's hand fall away from the knob as he swung round to face her. Once again she saw his astonishment. Once again she saw his blue eyes ablaze with passion. Once again Annabel experienced a surge of panic.

"A kiss is it?" he'd crooned with deceptive softness. "My sweet widgeon, I am at your service."

"N-n-never mind," she'd stuttered. "It was only a passing fancy."

"Lost your nerve have you? Never mind, little coward, I've enough for both of us."

His hands grasped her shoulders in a gentle vise. His hungry gaze locked on her mouth, as in slow increments he lowered his head and finally—just when she didn't think she could bear to wait a second longer—he'd kissed her. The instant their lips touched, Annabel felt all resistance melting.

His kiss left a sweet afterglow that tugged on her heartstrings as he led her back into the ballroom. Her thoughts skipped to the waltz they'd shared afterward. The way he'd held her had made her feel special. She'd wanted to dance on and on and never stop. Impossible, of course. Sooner or later, all dances ended.

When they'd parted, she'd been perfectly miserable until he returned to claim the supper dance. When that set ended, they'd gone into the supper room. Everything on her plate had tasted good. The champagne he'd poured for her tickled her nose.

Her thoughts reverted to the intimate kiss they'd shared. Beforehand, she'd expected it to be the same as their first, rather sweet, rather chaste. But their second kiss had been very different, which wasn't to say she'd been disappointed. The kiss was everything she'd hoped for in her feverish dreams. Yet, it was also more than she'd bargained for, because it had contained sensual overtones that had set in chain a yearning for even more kisses.

And, brazen hussy that she was, she had no regrets. The tip of her tongue outlined the contours of her generous mouth. Justin's kiss had aroused so many conflicting emotions it was hard to sort them out. While tender, the kiss he'd bestowed embodied more disturbing elements. How easily she'd yielded to the subtle pressure of lips that coaxed her to part them. How her breasts had grown taut as his tongue explored the moist contours of her mouth. And what of the searing heat that had scorched her loins before the kiss ended?

Annabel fanned her hot cheeks then smiled faintly. While matrimony was not her cup of tea, it had never been an ambition of hers to go through life unkissed. Whatever the future held, she'd always treasure the memory of the fiercely tender kiss they'd shared.

The sound of heavy drapes being shunted aside brought her back to the present with a jolt. Opening her eyes, the flood of sunlight momentarily blinded her.

"Good heavens! What time is it, Nancy?"

"Half past twelve, miss."

Annabel groaned. She felt like a slugabed, which was nonsensical. Most days she was up with the chickens. But it'd been two in the morning before she'd been able to seek her bed. Exhausted, she'd expected to fall asleep the instant her head met with her pillow. Unhappily, she'd been too excited. She'd lain there reliving the sizzling kiss they'd shared.

It'd been dawn before she'd finally drifted off, Annabel mused. Who would have guessed that a single kiss would have such a powerful effect on a supposedly confirmed spinster? For the first time, she was forced to question her suitability for the celibate life. If Justin's kiss were anything to go by, intimacy might lead to even more wondrous discoveries. So perhaps the marriage bed was not to be despised. Perhaps, too, it was the longing for children, coupled with the promise of physical fulfillment that persuaded innocent virgins to surrender their independence.

But enough of these fruitless musings! It was high time she faced the day ahead.

"Nancy, I'm devilishly sharp set. Fetch me a tray."

"Very good, miss."

The maid was about to scoot through the open door

when Annabel added, "While you're at it, send in my abigail."

An hour later, she'd breakfasted and donned a round dress of pomona green poplin. Her abigail was brushing her hair when Fanny burst into her bedchamber.

"About time you woke. The drawing room is abrim with bouquets from admirers."

Annabel shrugged. "It is no bread or butter of mine. Have someone put them in water and cease plaguing me."

Fanny grinned. "My, my! You are rather cross this morning. Correction. Make that afternoon."

"Give over, Fanny. I'm in no mood to be teased."

"Woke up on the wrong side of the bed, did you?"

"Not exactly. I'm cross because I overslept."

"Useless to fret. Come. The drawing room is packed with *your* admirers come to pay homage."

"Surely you jest?"

Fanny shook her head. "It is the truth. You've received so many bouquets the place smells like a hothouse."

"Bloody hell!" Annabel exclaimed.

Bless Fanny for warning her, Annabel thought. From the minute she set foot inside the packed drawing room, she'd felt like a tinned sardine. Tempted to flee, her scruples kept her rooted to the carpet. Her sole consolation being that, while it was considered polite to pay a courtesy call the day after a ball, it was deemed improper to stay longer than a half hour. Surely, Annabel reasoned, she could put up with these misguided puppies for thirty minutes, could she not?

As things turned out, she didn't have to because Justin materialized, brashly claiming she'd agreed to go for a drive with him.

Admittedly, it was hardly a day to venture abroad de-

pite the bright sun, but she could not bear to be trapped
nside with her so-called admirers another minute.

"Brought my curricle. Dress warmly," he called softly
s she hurried upstairs.

Inside her bedchamber, Annabel's abigail helped her
nistress exchange white kid slippers for sturdier half
oots and slip her arms into a white kerseymere spencer
hat covered the bodice of her pomona green gown and
vould afford added protection against catching pneu-
nonia from the wind.

Dismissing her dresser, Annabel plunked her green
noss silk bonnet on her head and tied its green and
vhite ribbands securely under her chin. To be sure,
[ustin had seen it before but it matched her gown. Besides, she was in a tearing hurry. She stuffed York tan
gloves into a deep pocket of her fur-lined cloak, then
went to join Justin at the foot of the stairs.

"Shall I need this?" she asked, indicating her cloak
draped over her arm.

He nodded. "Allow me."

Justin whisked the cloak off her crooked arm and
settled it about her shoulders before turning her to face
him. Gazing down at her enigmatically, he fastened the
braided frog closure situated at the hollow of her throat.
A cozy warmth filled Annabel. He made her feel safe
and protected.

"There. You should be warm enough."

"I trust so. Bundled up as I am, one would think I'm
about to embark for the Arctic Circle rather than a drive
in the park," she observed wryly.

"The wind has a nasty bite. I prefer not to take
chances with your health." He tucked her hand in his.
"Shall we go? I don't like to keep my prized bays cool-
ing their hooves any longer than necessary."

At the curb she took a minute to admire the handsome equipage. The curricle's neatly rounded body was

painted a deep forest green. It had black rimmed
wheels with bright yellow spokes.

"What a smart carriage! Is it new?"

"No. I bought it second-hand at a very good price if
I say so myself."

"Oh? However did you pay? Um . . . never mind. 'Tis
none of my business."

He chuckled. "No, it isn't. But such a paltry consid-
eration would hardly weigh with you."

"I never meant to be rude. Money matters fascinate me."

He grinned. "I'm more amused than offended. To
answer your question, I sold two Lely's."

She lifted an eyebrow. "At this rate, your walls will
be stripped bare in no time."

He gave a shout of laughter but, once recovered, said
coolly, "They already are at the town house. I found
the Lely's in the family vault at Camden Manor—a place
my cousin loathed and seldom visited. But enough of
my crass problems. Allow me to make Simon known to
you. The lad's my tiger."

Rigged out in dark green livery trimmed with gold
braid, and seated on a small perch above the rear
springs, Simon evidently served at the earl's pleasure as
combination groom and errand boy.

"Pleased to meet you, Simon," said Annabel.

The lad colored up and mumbled incoherently. She
cast Justin a quizzical look. He responded with a bland
smile that she found exasperating.

"Here, let me give you a hand up."

As he swung her up onto the carriage seat, an icy
curl of wind slipped beneath her billowing cloak. Once
seated, Annabel wrapped it more tightly about her slim
form. Shivering, she winged a grateful glance up to the
carriage's leather top that served as wind buffer. The
top could be lowered in fine weather but, of course,
today it was raised.

Justin scrambled up onto the driver's seat and took up the reins. But before he set the pair in harness in motion, he glanced at his companion and said in an undertone, "Don't fret about the boy. He's shy until he gets to know you. Once he does, there's no shutting him up."

"I see. Where are we bound?"

"I thought we'd drive to Berkeley Square and park under the trees across from Gunter's. I'll send Simon to fetch three hot chocolates. Is that agreeable?"

"Sounds delightful. Such an original notion. By the by, thank you for rescuing me last night from Lady Holland and this afternoon from my gentlemen callers."

"My pleasure. Allow me to continue mapping our itinerary. After we have warmed ourselves, I mean to dispatch Simon so that you and I may have a serious chat."

"My lord, you pique my curiosity. What on earth are we to discuss?"

The earl shot her a harried glance. "Later, my dear. Little pitchers have big ears."

"Just how do you propose to get rid of your tiger? Need I remind you drowning is a hanging offense?"

Her droll hectoring surprised a chuckle from him. "As I've no wish to end up the chief entertainment at Tyburn, I shall dispatch the lad to Hoby's in Bond Street to pick up my new boots. That should keep him out of our way until we've both had our say."

With a deft flick of his wrists, he set the matched pair in motion. Annabel could not begin to imagine what he wished to discuss and kept darting surreptitious glances at him, hoping to pick up clues. Seemingly oblivious to her scrutiny, Justin concentrated on moving the curricle forward despite the wind's opposition. But while he made some headway, she sensed his rate of progress displeased him.

Annabel deemed it wise to hold her tongue. After all, he was obviously out of temper. And the last thing she wished to be was a scapegoat.

Twenty-two

In summer, a grove of tall trees in full leaf provided shade for those patrons who preferred to park their carriages beneath them and send a footman into Gunter's to fetch ices. In winter, most patrons dined indoors where they eschewed ices in favor of turtle soup made from turtles shipped from Honduras.

But Justin was made of sterner stuff. Lusty October breeze notwithstanding, he hoped Annabel would not gainsay his plan to hold their discussion out in the open. To be candid, he could not bear the thought of anyone overhearing what he had to say.

As he drove past number seven Berkeley Square, Annabel exclaimed, "Gracious! Gunter had best take down his sign before the wind knocks it down."

Justin glanced toward the famed confectioner's pot and pineapple sign. "It's taking a drubbing, but I doubt the wind's strong enough to tear it loose from its moorings."

Annabel shot him a dubious look but said nothing. He halted his bays across the street from the swinging sign, pleased to note the same trees that provided shade in summer acted today as a wind buffer. Of course, it was not yet winter. But tell that to some poor chap with chilblains, thought Justin, as he sent Simon off to fetch three mugs of hot chocolate.

Once he'd gone, Justin lifted a seat cushion and pulled out a lap robe that he tucked around Annabel.

"There. Can't have you taking a chill, can I?"

"Little danger of that. I'm warm as toast."

Simon soon reappeared with three steaming mugs of milk chocolate topped off with a generous dollop of whipped cream.

"Heavenly!" cried Annabel after a sip.

Justin drained his mug and prayed for courage. During his years in the army, he'd never run from battle. But this was a different sort of engagement. This was a battle for Annabel's heart and soul and he desperately wanted to present his argument in winning terms. Though, of course, no matter what he said, there were no guarantees.

"Oim done, Cap'n," said Simon. "Shall I pop off to 'oby's?"

"Yes. Take Bruton Street. That way, should we finish our discussion early, I can meet you."

Justin waited until the lad disappeared from sight before he aimed an uneasy glance at Annabel and confessed, "I don't know quite where to begin."

"You are being very mysterious, my lord."

"Do you know what I like least about inheriting an earldom is being my lorded to death. Sounds so damned pompous," he grumbled.

Annabel laughed. "Hard luck. It is the proper way to address you."

"Blister the title! Friends use each other's given name. Do they not?"

"I suppose so."

"Can we not be friends?"

Annabel cast him a teasing glance. "Is no sacrifice too great to get your own way? Amazing."

"Do not mock me. I truly wish to establish a warm friendship between us."

"Friendships take time. We've not known each other very long, have we?"

"I beg to differ. Three years is more than ample."

"Do you take me for a flat? During those years, most of the time you were in Portugal and I, in England."

"Yes, well I'd have been close at hand more often, had it been possible," he said lamely. Then in a stronger, more confident voice he added, "Besides, it's not the length of time we've known each other that matters. It's how we feel about each other. It's about offering comfort when your friend is down in the dumps."

"I would imagine such friendships are rare. But nothing ventured, nothing gained. Why don't we give it a try?" Annabel suggested.

Justin's lungs were about to burst. He gulped in air in greedy gasps. Her answer had been of such vital importance, he'd been holding his breath without realizing it.

"My lord, are you feeling all the thing?"

He glowered. "For the love of heaven, spare me any more my lords. My name is Justin. Use it!"

"My lord, I—"

"Justin," he insisted through clenched teeth.

"Do you think to browbeat me? Some friendship!" she scoffed.

Devil a bit! Time to eat humble pie, he acknowledged.

"My dear Miss Drummond, I didn't mean to bully you. It's just that Annabel is such a pretty name. I long to use it. I cannot bear for my stupid title to stand in the way of our friendship."

"My lord, that is all very well, but—"

"One more my lord and I shall end up in bedlam. Is that what you want?"

"Well no, but . . ."

"It is settled then. You shall call me Justin and I shall call you Annabel."

Annabel's effort to look stern dissolved in a bout of helpless laughter. "Such persistence! I feel like I've been flattened by a mail coach."

He grinned. "Whatever it takes."

Annabel's gaze drew pensive. "But surely you didn't arrange our tete á tete just to persuade me to quit using your title. Or did you?"

"Of course not. But I'm not sure I'd ever have worked up the nerve to broach the subject, had you not begged a kiss at last night's ball."

Annabel bristled. "Must you keep harping on that string?"

Justin bit back a laugh. The adorable little hoyden *was* blushing. And so she should be. Her conduct had been outrageous—but also revealing of the passionate nature lurking beneath her serene surface. And in all candor, Justin conceded that passion was important to him. Not for him a wife with the sensibilities of a cold fish! Annabel was a warm-blooded delight.

Annabel fanned her hot cheeks. "La, sir, spare me my blushes. I can't think what got into me to behave so wickedly."

"Oh, surely not so very wicked," he teased. "Here I've been hoping against hope that I'd not seen the last of the brazen little hussy!"

Annabel flushed scarlet. "Sir, you are despicable! Take me home at once!"

Highly amused, he struggled to keep a straight face.

"What? After all the trouble I took to lure you to a secluded spot on the off chance you might wish to make further advances. Surely my dearest friend would not be so cruel."

"Wouldn't I just?" she fumed. "You, sir, are a cad of the first water."

Justin tossed back his head and gave a roar of laughter. He laughed until tears ran down his cheeks and his entire body was limp.

"Pax, Annabel, I was only joking. Lord, I haven't laughed so hard since Waterloo. In fact, I'm weak from it."

"A joke? You consider me a figure of fun?"

One glimpse of the pain in her eyes and Justin was tempted to shoot himself. "No such thing! My word on it!" he averred contritely. "I'm truly sorry. I should have kept tighter rein on my deplorable sense of humor. But you are such a delight to tease."

"Fie on you, sir! It is too bad of you to roast me."

"Just so. Am I forgiven?"

"Only if you promise to mend your ways in future."

"I so promise," he said solemnly.

"See that you do, sir," she admonished, gruffly. "Else our friendship is ended before it gets off the ground!"

Justin slowly released the breath he'd been holding. He'd earned a temporary reprieve, which was probably the best he could hope for after making a cake of himself by laughing like a demented hyena.

However, while he'd frittered away precious time, the afternoon had been waning. He must quit stalling. Justin nervously cleared his throat.

"Miss Drummond, that is, Annabel, I wish to pose a serious question. But before I do, I wish to make it clear that I don't expect an immediate answer. I prefer you think over my offer carefully, before you decide. Is that understood?"

"Your offer? Such an ominous phrase. Surely you don't intend to drop down on one knee and ask for my hand? I thought I'd made my views on marriage clear."

"I thought you had as well," he admitted with rueful candor. "Until last night, when you begged a kiss. I'm a gambler at heart. And with all due respect, I'm con-

vinced you are not nearly as faint hearted as you think
you are in regard to marriage."

Annabel sighed. "Dear me! Who would have thought
one kiss would stir up such a fuss. But there you stood,
you handsome devil, tempting me as the serpent
tempted Eve. You looked so dashing in your evening
dress, the impulse was well nigh irresistible. Even so, I
quite see I must beg your pardon for misleading you."

A needle-sized sword of poignant tenderness pierced
Justin's yearning heart. If only he could somehow persuade her to marry him, he'd do everything in his
power to make her happy, but he had a ways to go yet
on a perilous journey littered with rocky shoals.

"Do you accept my apology?" Annabel asked.

"I see no reason not to."

"Good! I'd much rather we be friends than marry
and quarrel."

"If I had my druthers, I'd like to be both friend and
husband."

"Please, Justin, no more importuning."

"Patience, my sweet. I'm almost done."

Annabel sighed. "In that case, pray continue."

Swallowing a triumphant smile, Justin told himself it
would never do to grow too cocky.

"I collect one of your objections to marriage is that
control of your assets would revert to your husband. If
you consent to marry me, I'm willing to leave you in
charge of both your merchant fleet and your fortune.
It would all be spelled out in the marriage settlement
so there'd be no misunderstanding later."

Annabel's jaw dropped. "What? Are you actually willing to let me keep my independence."

"Absolutely!" Justin paused to draw a deep breath.
"To me, marriage is the melding of two souls and two
bodies. In that sense, we'd become one. But financially
speaking, I don't want your bloody fortune. Marry me,

nd I'll let you be the financial wizard in the family.
hould I ever accumulate enough surplus capital to in-
est, I'll probably seek your advice. Mind you, putting
ny country estate in order will be a long struggle—even
f I sell the town house. But I'm confident with the
conomies I've already instituted, eventually Camden
Manor will flourish."

Distress clouded her deep blue eyes. "Mercy! How
ould I have been so mistaken in your character? I
ould have sworn the reason you came courting was to
ecover the four thousand pounds Papa won in his
reach of promise suit. Can you ever forgive me?"

The temptation to blame Boswell for putting the idea
nto his head in the first place was strong, but he firmly
esisted it. Even stronger was the temptation to not be
ompletely candid, but Justin knew he'd feel unworthy
nless he remained scrupulously honest. He also felt
e'd gain nothing lasting if he won her consent, but
ost his honor.

"There is nothing to forgive. Your instincts did not
ail you. Initially, regaining the four thousand pounds
ny cousin paid out did cross my mind. But once I had
chance to mull things over, I realized that justice had
een served. After all, your father advanced the exact
mount as partial payment of your dowry. When my
ousin jilted you, he forfeited any right to the money."

"But if that's how you felt why continue to pursue
ne?"

Justin, who'd been perspiring profusely, now broke
ut in a cold sweat. God's life, he commiserated, paying
ne's addresses was torture pure and simple. When he
ried to speak, his voice cracked. A damnable embar-
assment. Gritting his teeth, he pressed doggedly on.

"Because," he averred huskily, "I love you to distrac-
ion. No other reason, I swear it! My dearest Annabel,

will you please put me out of my misery and conse
to be my wife?"

She eyed him warily. "I thought you wished me t
mull things over before I gave you my answer."

Justin emitted a shaky sigh. "So I did, sweethear
Very well then, take your time. I daresay I can endu
being splayed on the rack a bit longer."

Three hours later, Annabel sat at her dressing tabl
smiling dreamily at her reflection. Her fingertip
brushed her swollen lips and a look of wonder shor
from her eyes as her thoughts tumbled backward to tha
afternoon.

At Berkeley Square she'd noted the lengthening sha
ows and shivered. Justin who'd just picked up the rein
dropped them, and turned to her, his concern etche
on his face.

"You're cold. I should be sentenced to fifty lashes f
dragging you out here, but I . . ."

Annabel covered his mouth with her gloved han
"Hush. Don't be so hard on yourself. I'm not *that* cold

Passion glittered in the depths of his pale blue ey
as he gently pulled her hand from his lips. "In th
case, I may have a remedy. Mind if I put it to the test

"You talk in riddles. A little plain speaking wou
not go amiss."

His eyes had held an impish gleam. "Actions spe
louder than words. What could be plainer?"

Gazing into her looking glass, a trace of a smile ill
minated Annabel's features. Quick as a wink, the rog
had stripped off her York tan glove and planted a pa
sionate kiss inside her wrist. The sensuous salute ha
caused her pulse rate to skip, then accelerate. Claimi
her mouth, he'd kissed her until her lips were swolle

At last, he'd lifted his head and looked her square in her eyes.

"Cold still?"

Cold? To the contrary, she'd felt like a raging furnace. She'd rather die than admit it, yet she suspected he knew, because he'd given a deep, masculine chuckle and kissed the tip of her nose before he picked up the reins and set off for Russell Square.

The dinner gong scattered her thoughts. Tonight, her silk gown was a delicate pearl gray trimmed with gold that set off her titian locks to perfection. Doubtless, if Justin were dining with her, he'd rain compliments on her already muddled head as effortlessly as he'd rained kisses on her face, neck and throat in Berkeley Square. Audacious rogue.

Rising, Annabel left her bedchamber. Lord Adam would dine with them—an event that would no doubt make Fanny sparkle. She was glad her dearest companion was so happy, but it did sadden Annabel that the couple planned to settle in Dorset where Adam intended to raise thoroughbreds on the land he'd inherited.

Ah well, it couldn't be helped. Annabel supposed she'd get used to Fanny's defection in time. But gracious, it would be lonely in London without her.

As to Justin's marriage proposal, she honestly didn't know what to think. She kept vacillating between marriage and the status quo. Annabel paused at the foot of the stairs, deep in thought. From what she'd gleaned from his conversation, Justin planned to settle at Camden Manor near Rye. That would present logistic problems for her, since she had no idea how to operate a merchant fleet from the country.

Perhaps, though, he'd allow her to keep this town house open so she could fly up to London whenever necessary. But even if he permitted it, she had only so much energy and there were only so many hours in the day. What would happen if she had a child? Or two, or three? Not that she didn't want children. She did. Indeed, one reason she was seriously considering plunging into matrimonial seas was her desire to hold a babe in her arms. Naturally, the child wouldn't be entirely hers. It would belong to Justin, too. But that didn't bother her. She felt he'd be a good father.

She had other concerns as well. She'd been born in London and rarely traveled further than its outskirts. What if country life didn't suit her?

It was all Justin's fault that her thoughts were in such a muddle, she thought crossly. Bad enough that she'd begged him to kiss her at the ball. In good conscience she couldn't blame him for taking her up on her offer. Still, it had been a scatterbrained notion. One, if she had a grain of sense, she'd regret.

The problem was she didn't regret the kiss they'd shared at the ball—nor those he'd bestowed only a few hours earlier. Indeed, if she didn't mend her wanton ways, she'd land in the suds for sure.

Should she marry Justin or remain a spinster? She hated to vacillate. Yet she couldn't decide. Even worse, she had a sneaky suspicion that Justin had her pegged right when he'd said she didn't know her own mind.

Until she did, she must bide her time, which for someone with Annabel's impatient nature, would be, to say the least, a trial.

Twenty-three

Inside Lloyd's Coffee House, Annabel glanced across the high backed-booth at her long-time friend and occasional mentor, Nathan Rothschild. Justin had flattered her when he'd referred to her as a financial wizard. If anyone deserved the accolade it was Nathan.

Now, Rothschild studied Annabel's face. "Vy so blue-deviled? A nobleman vishes to marry you. You say he lufs you and you luf him. So vat is der problem?"

"He's not very rich. Unless I help him, it'll take years to put his country estate on a profitable footing."

"Years? Vit your fortune? You are pulling mine foot, yes?"

"I'm not sure I wish to finance the repairs."

"Vy not? Your children vil inherit, yes?"

"Yes, of course. I'm not thinking clearly. Of course I shall help put the place back in good heart. But Mr. Rothschild, there are other problems."

"Mine Gott! You have a goot head on your shoulders. Vy not use it, instead of inventing pitholes? Unless you don't vish to marry der earl and are only toying vit him."

"Toy with Justin? I wouldn't dare. Besides, I do love him. It's just that I'm London bred. I'm not sure I can adapt to country life."

"Mine dear Miss Annabel, I vil now talk to you like a Dutch uncle, yes?"

Annabel nodded.

"Goot. From vat you have told me, I tink he is a goot man. He vil give you vat most men vil not—namely, control of your fortune. Vat more can you vant?"

Annabel gave a nervous giggle. "You make me sound like a silly widgeon. Wish me happy. I'm about to embark on the biggest gamble of my life. I've decided to wed Justin Camden, eleventh Earl of Summerfield."

"Goot!" Rothschild reached across the table to pat her hand avuncularly.

"And now, my dear friend, I believe I shall go home and consider how best to inform him of my decision."

She rose to her feet. Rothschild hastily followed suit, since it was considered rude to remain seated in a lady's presence. Yet no sooner had Annabel risen than she sank back into the seat she'd just vacated, ashen faced.

"Mine Gott! Vat is wrong? You are pale as a ghost."

"Blast! I forgot all about Kenneth Boswell. He's Justin's solicitor but I don't trust him. Oh, Nathan, what on earth am I going to do?"

"You vil talk it over vit your earl and come to an understanding, yes?"

"Quite right! And the sooner the better! Will you excuse me, Nathan?"

She tried to rise, but her plan was thwarted by Rothschild, whose grip on her hand kept her seated. "Stay vere you are, child. I'll fetch him. Just remember, verds spoken in anger can vound."

In a booth across the coffee room, Justin's harried solicitor radiated disapproval.

"Let me get this straight," Kenneth Boswell said, his voice dripping with acid. "You wish me to draw up a codicil to your will leaving all your worldly goods to Miss Drummond. In addition, you wish stipulated in the marriage settlement papers that she shall retain sole control of both her fortune and her merchant fleet, correct?"

Justin cast him a cool smile. Unhappily, Kenneth's rubbery code of ethics had cast a blight on their relationship. And if Boswell gave him too much sauce, he'd find another solicitor.

"Letter perfect. How long will it take you to produce these documents?"

"When do you need them?"

"The sooner the better."

Boswell gave a derisive chuckle. "Very well, but it'll cost you extra."

Justin's eyes hardened. "Don't toy with me, Kenneth. If I don't receive the required documents in a timely fashion, I shall be forced to—"

"Ach, pardon mine interruption, gentlemen."

Boswell flicked an impatient glance at the lean gentleman with an aquiline nose, who'd had the gall to insinuate himself into a privileged conversation. Then, in a wink of an eye, recognition dawned and rancor was replaced by unabashed awe.

Scrambling to his feet, the solicitor scurried to mend his fences. "Well met, Mr. Rothschild. How may I serve you, sir?"

The man's shrewd eyes took his measure. "Vun small favor. Introduce me to dis gentleman."

Boswell's eyes looked on the verge of popping as he turned toward his amused client, who'd now risen to his feet.

"Justin, allow me to make known to you Nathan Rothschild, London's foremost financial genius. Mr. Rothschild, permit me to introduce the Earl of Summerfield."

Once they'd shaken hands, Justin smiled and said, "Won't you join us, sir?"

"Nein. Der lady vil have mine head for vashing if I detain you."

"Lady?"

Eyes twinkling, Rothschild nodded. "Miss Drummond."

Justin's brow cleared. "Ah, Annabel. Where is she, sir?"

"Across der vay. She vishes a private verd vit you."

Justin grinned at Rothschild. "I'm on my way, sir."

His eyes alive with mischief, Justin dodged a scurrying waiter en route to his rendezvous with Annabel. Reaching her booth, he slid into the opposing seat and shot her a devil may care grin.

"My dear Annabel, fancy meeting you here."

"It's one of my haunts. Besides, I am not your dear," she said crossly.

"What's wrong?"

"Wrong? Not a blessed thing!"

He cast his eyes ceilingward. *Lord, grant me patience!* he silently pleaded. "My dear, Annabel, if I've offended you, you've only to tell me how and I shall endeavor to make amends."

"Ha!" Annabel scoffed.

"Sweetheart," he hissed. "Are you perchance trying to drive me round the bend."

"Who me? Why should I do that?" Her feigned innocence crumbled in the face of his relentless probing. "Very well, Justin, for all the good it'll do me, I shall tell you!"

"Excellent!" He cocked his head to one side, his demeanor expectant. When she did not choose to enlighten him immediately, he silently counted to ten. "Annabel, Rothschild said you wished a word with me. If you've changed your mind, be so good as to tell me, so that I may resume my business."

"You mean with Kenneth Boswell, do you not?"

He nodded, suddenly wary.

"He was once my man of business. I dismissed him three years ago because I could no longer trust him."

"Yes, I know."

Her dark blue eyes brimmed with disillusionment. "I had to."

"I understand how you must have felt. I can't say I blame you. In your shoes, I daresay I'd have done the same."

Annabel visibly brightened. "Oh good! I was so afraid you would not understand the necessity."

"Well, you may now put those fears to rest!" Justin awarded her a loving smile. "Now then, if that is all, may I escort you to your carriage?"

"No wait! I wish to discuss your meeting."

"You wish to know the nature of my discussion?"

She shook her head. "No. I wish to discuss Boswell's lack of character."

A premonition gripped him. "His character?" he asked with sinking heart.

"Yes," she whispered. "You see, I've all but made up my mind to accept your flattering offer of marriage, but there is bad blood between me and Boswell. Now do you understand?"

Justin gripped the underside of the table until his fingers went numb, but when he spoke he took care not to let any sign of his inner turmoil escape.

"I won't insult your intelligence by pretending I don't. I do sympathize with you, my dear. It will make for an awkward situation to be sure. But Annabel, Kenneth and I have been friends since our bluecoat days. He's always been scrupulously honest in his dealings with me. So, I can't quite see on what grounds I can dismiss him."

"To my mind, such an arrangement would be intolerable. Cannot you tell him you are turning him off for my sake?"

Justin released a long tortured sigh. "To be sure there is nothing to stop me from dismissing him without cause, save my scruples. Please, dearest, can you not find it your heart to forgive him?"

"Forgive him? Certainly not!"

"Well, I don't wish to be unreasonable. But surely you can bring yourself to overlook our connection. After all, I need a man of business to handle my affairs."

"What? Tolerate that mealy mouthed turncoat! Never!"

"A pretty kettle of fish!" he exclaimed, clearly disgusted. "What now, I wonder?"

"Justin, I detest ultimatums. But, simply put, you must choose. Do you wish to marry me or do you wish to retain your solicitor?"

"Devil a bit! Don't ask this of me, sweetheart. Pray do not."

"Choose!" she demanded. "Him or me!"

Justin's pale blue eyes iced over. "Annabel, I may love you to distraction but I won't climb into Lord Holland's boots for you—not for all the tea in China."

"Have your wits gone abegging? What does Lord Holland have to do with this discussion?"

"Damn your eyes, woman! He has everything to do with it. Lord Holland is Lady Holland's husband."

"Is he indeed," Annabel said sarcastically. "Naturally, that explains everything!"

"No, it doesn't but you may be sure I mean to," Justin promised grimly. "Once upon a time Holland was a dashing young buck. But after a few years under the cat's paw, his peers have lost all respect for him and he's become the butt of their jokes. All because he allows Lady Holland to lead him round by the ring in his nose. So no, my dearest Annabel, I won't sack Kenneth Boswell to please you. And most definitely, no, I will not be your lap dog."

A terrible black chasm yawned between them. A chasm Justin acknowledged he dare not cross, lest he use all self-respect. But God almighty! The thought of coming so close to winning his true love only to lose her instead was heartbreaking.

"I seem to have touched a nerve, my lord. I do sincerely beg your pardon," said Annabel in a voice carefully stripped of emotion. "I'm sure you understand why I feel the best thing for both our sakes is for me to respectfully refuse your flattering offer."

"Hell and the Devil!" Justin raged. "Was it not enough that I bent over backwards to please you? My peers will think I've run mad, allowing my wife to manage her own affairs. I assented to your retaining control of your entire fortune, and a merchant fleet. Are you satisfied? Not by a long shot.

"You're right, Annabel. It would never work between us. Because while I loved you enough to respect your judgment, you balked at affording me the same courtesy. So farewell, my love. I'm off to Camden Manor where I intend to bury myself 'til hell freezes over."

Nostrils flaring, Justin spun on his heel and stormed across the coffee room toward the entrance. So enraged was he, he would've passed by the booth where Boswell and Rothschild sat conversing—had not the former caught hold of his coat sleeve.

"What's the rush, Justin? Come sit down so we can conclude our business."

"Later. Turn me loose."

Instead, Boswell tightened his grip and rose to his feet. "Not yet. You're in a rare taking. Sit down until you cool off."

"Devil take you! Unhand me!" Justin snarled.

"Now what kind of a friend would I be if I let you stalk off in high dudgeon?"

Justin gave a vicious tug, freeing his sleeve. His face an alarming puce, he balled his hands into tight fists. "In future, keep your bloody hands to yourself."

"Really, old chap, best you take a damper," Boswell

coaxed. "And while you're at it, why not unburden yourself?"

"Unburden myself? In what regard?"

"The little witch's latest demand. That's what put you in such a flame, is it not?"

Normally even-tempered, the slur on Annabel's character—by the very man whose defense he'd leapt to with such disastrous results—tipped the scales. Raising his fives, Justin drew Boswell's cork. Then, nimbly sidestepping the crumpled form at his feet, he awarded Rothschild a curt nod and stalked out of Lloyd's Coffee Room.

Mouth agape, Rothschild gazed at Justin's retreating figure then down at the floored solicitor.

"Mine Gott!"

A crowd of fluttering waiters flocked to the booth. Rothschild steadfastly ignored them, but when a physician showed up, he placed Boswell in his care and went to rejoin Annabel.

Sensing his presence, Annabel lifted her bowed head to reveal a tear-stained face. "Oh, Nathan," she wailed. "I've made such of botch of things."

He sank down onto the opposing bench. "Hush, mine child. Vy cry over spilt milk? Far better to find a vay to mend dis breach, yes?"

Heartened by his common sense, Annabel was quick to agree. He was such a dear, she reflected as she used the snowy white lawn handkerchief he offered to mop up her tears.

"Do you really think talking things over will help?"

He shrugged. "Vat can it hurt?"

Invited to open her budget, Annabel explained, "Justin is adamant about retaining Boswell's services. Even my last-ditch ultimatum failed to budge him."

Rothschild sighed. "Ultimatums are never vise. But I

vil not vaste time reading you a scold. Far better that
ve tink of a vay to mend matters, yes?"

"Quite right!"

Smiling faintly, Rothschild recalled how Boswell's reference to Annabel as "de little vitch" had put Justin in
such a taking, he'd planted him a facer. Only a man
disappointed in love would behave in such a skimble
skamble manner. However, he refrained from apprising
Annabel of what had occurred. Marriage required give
and take and he felt it imperative that she learn to be
a bit more pliable.

"Only tell me what I must do to win back Justin's
regard, and I swear I shall do it."

Rothschild's dark eyes twinkled. "Even if I advise you
to vait until tomorrow?"

"Wait? Oh but, sir, I've always heard it best not to
let the sun set on a quarrel."

"Gott grant me patience!"

"Sorry," Annabel said meekly.

"Vat happened ven you explained tings to der earl?"

"He agreed I had cause, but refused to sever his own
relationship with Boswell. He feels it unjust to dismiss
a man who has served him well for many years."

"Goot for him! You are a lucky voman. Der earl has
integrity."

"Humph! I might have known you'd take his side.
Men!"

"Ach, now ve come to der bone of contention. Ven he
refused to dismiss Bosvell, your feelings ver hurt, yes?"

"Most definitely, although Justin proclaimed my ultimatum the final straw. I wasn't trying to bully him. I
just wanted assurance that he valued me as he ought."

Her voice broke and a lone tear trickled down her
cheek.

"*Nein, nein,* mine child, you must not veep. You must
heed vat I say. Yes?"

Annabel did not trust herself to speak for fear she'd burst into tears so she settled for a vigorous nod.

"Goot! Now den, vat vould you do if he'd asked you to dismiss Miss Bolton?"

"Justin would never do that. He admires Fanny."

"Of course, he vil not ask this of you. But vat vould you do if he did?"

Annabel mulled this over, then cast him an impish grin. "I'd tell my lord earl to go to the devil!"

He cast her a sad, knowing smile. "Yet ven der shoe vas on der other leg, you did not allow him the same option. If you vish to handle your own business affairs, it is only fair dat you let Justin handle his, yes?"

The play of contradictory emotions upon Annabel's mobile features fascinated Rothschild. At last, she released a tortured sigh. "I gather you think I overstepped my bounds."

Rothschild responded with one of his eloquent shrugs.

"Oh blast! I suppose I must swallow my pride and tolerate Boswell, but I beg leave to tell you it goes sorely against the grain!"

"Ach, Miss Annabel, you are as clever as you are beautiful. Tomorrow you vil summon der earl and eat humble crow, yes?"

She nodded, then rose. "I fear I must be going. Thank you for your wise counsel."

"Ach, you vil allow me to escort you to your carriage, yes?"

Laughing, she agreed.

However, as her elegant carriage pulled away from the curb, Annabel couldn't help but wonder what she'd do, if after she'd made a cake of herself by apologizing, Justin then said he no longer wished to marry her.

Minutes later, she knew exactly what she'd do—she'd brain him!

Twenty-four

The following day Justin woke in his hotel room shortly after eleven o'clock with a headache acquired, he dimly recollected, in a vain attempt to drown his sorrows the night before. He thought of ordering MacTavish to make one of his wondrous hair of the dog concoctions that always worked like a charm. Then he remembered that Jamie was looking after things at Camden Manor, whilst his lovesick master traveled up to London to lay siege to fair Annabel's heart.

Annabel! Recalling their quarrel, Justin started to leap out of bed with the skipbrained intention of mending matters that very instant. Unhappily, the sudden jarring made his stomach queasy and his head spin. He was forced to lay completely immobile until the room ceased to whirl.

That stupid quarrel! His eyes glazed over. Lord save them, they'd make a spectacle of themselves by airing their dirty linen in public. He groaned. He fancied the fishmongers at Billingsgate showed more decorum. The memory of his punishing chop to Boswell's jawbone followed by a flush hit in his bread basket occasioned another groan.

Maybe he'd just lie there until he died of mortification. After all, what was so special about life now that he'd lost Annabel?

He stiffened. Hell and the Devil! What ailed him to

be mooning over the stubborn wench? He'd be damned if he'd budge on his principles. Under no circumstance would he be her lap dog.

He opened one eye. Nothing catastrophic occurred. Taking that as a good omen, he opened the other. Nothing for it, he decided. He must climb out of bed and go make his peace with Boswell before quitting town. As for Annabel, he feared they'd made such a botch of things there was no mending matters.

By one o'clock he'd managed to down a piece of dry toast and swallow a cup of green tea. Immaculately groomed, he was sauntering across Long's Hotel lobby, when an elderly porter intercepted him and handed him a sealed note.

"M'lord, should you care to write out a reply, the footman who brought this is waiting."

Intrigued, Justin raised the folded sheet to his nostrils. One sniff brought a smug, masculine smile to his lips. Recognizing Annabel's scent, he retired to a nearby alcove where he broke the seal and unfolded a single sheet of velum. He scanned the page, refolded the note and, grimfaced, filed it in a vest pocket.

What gall to summon him as if he were a common lackey! In a foul temper, he stormed into a small anteroom adjacent to the lobby, which had been set aside for letter writing. There, he seated himself at a writing table and dashed off a curt reply. Once sure the ink was dry, he folded the note in thirds and sealed it with a bit of heated candle wax imprinted with his signet ring. Exiting the writing room, he placed the missive in the hands of the waiting footman and bade him deliver it to his mistress.

Annabel was trying her best to concentrate on the open ledger before her when Fenton invaded the study, earing Justin's response on a pounded silver tray. Anxous to know its contents, she could barely contain her mpatience until he withdrew. Alone once more, she roke the seal and, her midnight blue eyes sparkling in nticipation of a joyous reconciliation, began to read.

She scanned it quickly. Blanching, she read it again, ach word of his elegant script a seeming death knell o all her hopes and dreams.

> My dear Miss Drummond,
> I regret to say I cannot spare the time to call in person as I plan to quit London within the hour, bound for my country estate in Rye. I am, Madam, your most obedient servant,
>
> Summerfield

Annabel remained in such a foul mood all day, no one lared disturb her. At least, not until Fanny scratched ightly on the study door, then entered with a sweet smile.

"Time to close the ledger, dearest. Fenton says you've een holed up for hours. Shall we adjourn to the drawng room?"

"No!" Annabel snapped.

Fanny's brown eyes took on the look of a wounded loe's. Swamped with guilt, Annabel hastened to add in a more conciliatory tone, "That is, I don't care for company."

Alerted by the melancholy note in Annabel's voice, Fanny took a closer look. Only then did it fully register that her friend sat slumped in the gold-striped wing chair with a note dangling from her limp hand.

"Dearest, you look as if your best friend died. What troubles you?"

Annabel responded with a mirthless titter. "What has died is Justin's regard for me."

"Don't be ridiculous. He adores you. If he hasn't tol]
you so yet, you must not repine. Mark my words. He'
about to pay his addresses."

"Fanny, you are behind times. He already did."

"Really? Why this is excellent news! Adam wishes ।
marry me sooner rather than later. I've hesitated ।
name a firm date since I wished to see your futur
settled first. But now all is in train, is it not?"

"Fanny, come down to earth," Annabel advise(
glumly. "Nothing whatsoever is in train."

"But . . . but I understood you to say that Summe|
field asked for your hand."

Annabel let out a great sigh. "So he did. I told hi|
I'd think about it. Then we quarreled."

"Did you? Well, never mind. I'm sure you'll soo
make up, will you not?"

Annabel shook her head. "I fear not. You see, w
quarreled over Boswell. I asked Justin to sack him. N(
only did he refuse, he accused me of meddling."

"Were you, dearest?" Fanny quizzed gently.

"I suppose I was. Something I wouldn't ordinaril
stoop to, but I so despise that scurvy fellow's conduct.

"Perfectly understandable. Still, I doubt all is los
provided, of course, you are willing to apologize."

"Lord knows I've tried. Earlier, I sent round a not
to him at Long's Hotel asking him to call. In my han|
I hold his written refusal. So you see, dearest, he n
longer wishes to marry me."

"Rubbish! You've only to starch up your courage an
call on him in person. Depend upon it! He'll be to(
flattered by your marked attention to refuse a person;
entreaty."

Expression woebegotten, Annabel's chin wobbled. "]
is too late, Fanny. He's already quit London and i
bound for his estate in Rye."

"So? Sussex is not at the ends of the earth, is it?"

"Truly, Fanny, there is no mending matters. Our quarrel was so bitter, all is in ruins between us."

"Nonsense! I'll travel with you to lend you countenance. Depend upon it, he'll be so pleased that you went to so much trouble to track him down, he'll happily listen."

"What. traipse all over the countryside to apologize to a reluctant swain? Never!"

"But, dearest—"

"Not another word," Annabel warned through her teeth. "I won't follow him to Rye and that's final!"

"Very well, dearest," Fanny said dejectedly. "I suppose you know your own business best."

"Most definitely!" Annabel agreed stoutly. "Now do run along. As you no doubt have already gathered, I'm in no mood for company."

Fanny emitted a resigned sigh that lingered in Annabel's ears long after she quit the room. Annabel stared into the flames, her expression sullen. A fall of coals produced a burst of sparks and startled her.

Redirecting her gaze, she regarded Justin's cruel note with loathing. Why hang on to it? She couldn't think of a single valid reason. Mind made up, she jumped to her feet and proceeded to tear his heartless response into miniscule pieces which she then tossed into the fire. Watching them burn, Annabel wished it were as easy to strip her mind of the treasure trove of memories of Justin—especially the ones that evoked her tendermost feelings. But, of course, such a wish could not be granted. Sadly, it seemed that she was destined to be haunted by memories of her beloved to the end of her days.

A week later, Justin emerged from Long's Hotel. He was not in the most sanguine frame of mind. Nonethe-

less, not one to sit about twiddling his thumbs, he was
soon strolling down Old Bond Street headed for
Mitchell's, a popular gathering place for young bucks.

Entering the combination bookseller and stationer,
he welcomed the buzz of a multitude of low-keyed conversations that proclaimed the establishment an accred-
ited bastion of masculine camaraderie. He'd come to
find something to read. Rather than spend the evening
gadding about town, he'd much prefer to spend it inside his hotel suite immersed with a gripping tale. Still,
he meant to be quick about it. The place was thick with
tobacco smoke that invariably caused his eyes to water
and sting should he linger too long.

He'd just purchased Scott's *Waverley* when he was
hailed by Lord Adam, whom he hadn't set eyes on since
the betrothal ball.

"Didn't expect to run into you here, old chap.
Thought you'd retired to Rye."

Justin gave a wry chuckle. "That was certainly my
intention. I was all set to go when my man of business
sent round a note asking me to stick around until the
final papers transferring ownership have been signed."

"House sold, did it?"

Justin nodded. "Now, do forgive me. My eyes sting
like the dickens from tobacco smoke. Call round tomorrow and we'll have a good chat."

Clad in a plum-colored woolen gown that offered an
interesting contrast to her titian hair, Annabel entered
the breakfast room. Fanny sat at the linen-swathed table,
reading.

"Your daily love letter, dearest?" she teased.

Fanny glanced up, her cheeks flushed, her eyes
dreamy. "Adam is most attentive. But today's missive is

not only a love letter. It contains an interesting tidbit
that can aid your cause."

"My cause? Dearest, must you be so melodramatic?"
Too even-tempered to take umbrage, Fanny gave a
good-natured laugh. "I am not exaggerating. It is truly
good news. Adam relates that Justin was forced to delay
his departure in order to complete a business transaction."

Annabel wrapped her off-white merino shawl more
tightly about her in the hope of warding off a sudden
chill that had absolutely nothing to do with the wintry
weather. *Was there ever such a contrary fellow?* she mused.
She'd thought him long gone. Instead, he was still in
town where she might have accidentally bumped into
him, which would undoubtedly have been awkward. Besides, had he truly cared for her, by now he'd have called
on her, eager to mend their quarrel. Instead, he'd been
careful to give her wide berth and, if she had a grain of
sense, she'd continue to do the same to him.

"The earl's whereabouts no longer interest me," she
averred coldly.

"Don't be a paper-skull!" Fanny admonished. "Here's
your chance to apologize in person. I shall lend you
countenance by accompanying you to Long's."

"Fanny, I am not so foolish as to wear my heart on my
sleeve. I shall not call on him and that's the end of it!"

His mood pensive, Justin descended the carpeted
stairs. Not a single day passed that he didn't think of
Annabel and wish he hadn't handled things with more
tact. Nor did a night pass that his dreams weren't
haunted by her elusive aura. Still there was no use crying,
was there?

Reaching the foot of the stairs, his intention was to

saunter across the lobby and exit through the front
door. But this plan was thwarted by a canny porter.

"Your lordship, a Miss Drummond desires a private
word in the writing room."

Instantaneously, Justin's spirits perked up. Smiling
coolly, he said, "Thank you. Here's something for your
trouble."

He handed him a half-crown and was halfway to his
destination before the lackey ceased groveling.

Justin paused at the threshold of the small anteroom
to admire his beloved's profile. Her glorious red tresses
shimmered in slanted rays of sunlight filtering through
a tall casement window. His breath caught in his throat
as she turned to face him.

"Justin. Thank goodness. I've been a fever of impatience."

"Well, here I am, entirely at your disposal."

"Excellent. But first I must dismiss Nancy."

Shifting her gaze to the maid who'd accompanied
her, she bade her wait in the carriage. But once the
servant had withdrawn, Annabel seemed tongue-tied.

"This is so awkward," she said at last. "I—I've come
to apologize."

At first, her husky voice could be clearly heard, but
to her dismay it faded to a whisper toward the finish.
Annabel felt her cheeks warming and gazed down at
her hands, willing them not to fidget. She must attain
better control of herself else he'd think her bird-witted.

Staring at the repentant hellcat's bowed head, an
enormous lump blocked Justin's throat. That she'd
been willing to brave his wrath and risk rejection was
all the assurance he needed that she truly cared for
him. In addition, he now felt rather small-minded for
having refused to honor her summons, thus making it
necessary for her to humble herself in a hotel lobby.

He blinked to clear suddenly blurred vision as he

sed one long, slender finger to raise her chin, thus
making it possible to gaze directly into her luminous
dark blue eyes.

"I own I am flattered, but I am equally curious. Why
do you feel you owe me an apology?"

"Countless reasons," she admitted ruefully. "First off,
I must beg pardon for turning a private tiff into a public
spectacle. I fear one of my worst faults is impetuosity."

"Never mind. I forgive you."

"I thank you, but I am nowhere near done. You'd
best not interrupt again, lest I lose my courage."

"By all means carry on, noble lioness."

"By far my worst transgression was demanding that
you dismiss Boswell and ripping up when you refused."

Actually, Justin reflected, her criticism of Boswell's
character was not so outrageous as he'd originally assumed. Oddly enough, although he'd been willing to
overlook the fact that Kenneth had urged him to take
the dishonorable course of wooing Annabel simply to
square accounts, Boswell had lacked the generosity to
excuse Justin's burst of temper that had resulted in the
cagey solicitor's black eye. They'd severed their business
arrangement then and there. Thus, it seemed his adorable bride was not going to have to suffer Boswell's presence after all, Justin silently acknowledged. Even so, she
must be made to understand that he'd brook no inter-
ference in his personal business.

"To interfere in your business dealings was very
wrongheaded of me and I beg your forgiveness," Annabel continued.

Elation made him light-headed. Beaming, he hastened to say, "Which I freely grant. Done now?"

"Not quite. I also wish to say I love and respect you
and hope these sentiments are reciprocated. Are they?"

Justin cast her a rakish grin. "Absolutely! Care for a
demonstration?"

Pinkening, Annabel shook her head vigorously. "Pra:
spare me my blushes. To put on yet another public dis
play would surely sink me beyond the pale."

"See here, sweetheart. Just because all is forgive:
doesn't mean I'm letting you off Scot free. I deman(
a forfeit."

Alarm flickered in her dark blue irises. "W-what sor
of a forfeit?"

"Nothing major," he assured her gruffly. "First off
I'm going to steal a kiss or two. Then you and I ar(
driving straight to Doctor's Commons so I can obtai:
a special license. Any objection?"

"Rather highhanded, is it not?"

Justin went completely still. "Annabel, if you don'
wish to marry me, tell me straight-away. I don't thin|
my battered heart can take any more shilly shallying."

"I can't think what you mean. I've wanted to be you:
wife from the instant I saw you sprawled at my feet."

"And I, my darling, wanted to take you in my arm:
and cherish you forever the day my cousin jilted you a'
St. George's Chapel."

"Did you really?"

His blood singing in his veins, he nodded solemnly
his eyes brimming with love.

"Well then, my dearest slowtop, I suggest you ceas(
to shilly shally and kiss me."

"So I shall, my brazen little hussy. So I shall."

Silence reigned as he made good his promise.